SPECIAL MESSAGE TO READERS

This book is published under the auspices of

THE ULVERSCROFT FOUNDATION

(registered charity No. 264873 UK)

Established in 1972 to provide funds for research, diagnosis and treatment of eye diseases. Examples of contributions made are: —

A Children's Assessment Unit at Moorfield's Hospital, London.

•

Twin operating theatres at the Western Ophthalmic Hospital, London.

•

A Chair of Ophthalmology at the Royal Australian College of Ophthalmologists.

•

The Ulverscroft Children's Eye Unit at the Great Ormond Street Hospital For Sick Children, London.

You can help further the work of the Foundation by making a donation or leaving a legacy. Every contribution, no matter how small, is received with gratitude. Please write for details to:

THE ULVERSCROFT FOUNDATION,
The Green, Bradgate Road, Anstey,
Leicester LE7 7FU, England.
Telephone: (0116) 236 4325

In Australia write to:
THE ULVERSCROFT FOUNDATION,
c/o The Royal Australian and New Zealand
College of Ophthalmologists,
94-98 Chalmers Street, Surry Hills,
N.S.W. 2010, Australia

DREAM OF DANGER

Recently widowed, following a marriage of convenience, Madeleine Corning grieves for the loss of her baby son. She's grateful for the protection of her late husband's cousin, Cornelius, although her loyal servant Ellen believes he's not trustworthy — and that her child still lives. Should Madeleine turn to stranger William Franklyn for help — but why has he been watching her house? And he is not the only one, it seems. She must undergo danger and treachery to unravel the truth.

Books by Anne Hewland
in the Linford Romance Library:

STOLEN SECRET
TO TRUST A STRANGER
A SUBTLE DECEIT
BLIGHTED INHERITANCE
A DANGEROUS REFUGE

ANNE HEWLAND

DREAM OF DANGER

Complete and Unabridged

LINFORD
Leicester

First published in Great Britain in 2011

First Linford Edition
published 2012

British Library CIP Data

Hewland, Anne.
Dream of danger. - -
(Linford romance library)
1. Love stories.
2. Large type books.
I. Title II. Series
823.9′2–dc23

ISBN 978–1–4448–1216–9

Published by
F. A. Thorpe (Publishing)
Anstey, Leicestershire

Set by Words & Graphics Ltd.
Anstey, Leicestershire
Printed and bound in Great Britain by
T. J. International Ltd., Padstow, Cornwall

This book is printed on acid-free paper

1

Surely that was dear Ellen's voice? No, that was impossible. Her maidservant had been absent from her sickroom for days now — even weeks. She must be dreaming. Dreams could bring hope; better by far than waking to despair.

'Miss Madeleine! You must listen to me. Your child may still be alive.'

Madeleine knew now that this was a dream. Ellen had gone, and just when she needed her most. She remembered what had happened, all too well — and wished she did not. She was no longer Miss Madeleine. She was Mrs Oliver Corning, lately widowed. And their child, her dearest infant son, had died too. That was what they had told her.

She turned her head on the pillow. 'I just want to sleep. To forget.'

'No.' Ellen was whispering urgently. 'This is important. Do not drink your hot chocolate. But let the nurse think that you have. You must pour it away.'

What nonsense was this? But, she thought, it was probably best not to argue with dream people. Madeleine smiled weakly. 'Pour it away? How?'

'If you raise yourself — so — and lean over just a little — see, there? A gap between the floorboards. You can reach that.'

'But it will show underneath.'

Perhaps this was real, after all. Her mouth was dry.

'I thought of that. It will only go into the old broom cupboard on the floor below and I have set a bucket at the back, in there. No one will notice. Do that every time. Drink only water or lemonade. And I think the soup will be all right.' She stroked Madeleine's forehead. 'I hate to see you like this. But I will come back later and hope to find you much better.'

'My baby — what did you mean?'

Madeleine was beginning, but somewhere a door banged and Ellen jerked away.

'I must go. Pretend you are still doped and sleepy. With everyone — but the nurse in particular.' And Ellen was gone.

Madeleine sank back onto her pillows and closed her eyes. She would hardly have to pretend to be weary. A very strange dream, but better than most of the nightmares that tormented her, based on the horrible and inescapable truth. This was the time of day when memory was at its clearest and she would often wake sweating, able to recall everything that had happened. Fortunately it never seemed to last. Once she had drunk her chocolate, her head became clouded once more. And she had learned almost to welcome the blessed forgetfulness.

Could one become ill with grief? That must be what had happened. And the cruelty of Oliver's unfathomable rejection and the onset of her own illness before first her baby was gone, and then Oliver.

Or had he died first? Difficult to remember. She had not been allowed to hold her baby for one last time, despite her tears and pleading.

It was all a confusion. Best not to try and remember. Not until she was well. Ellen was right. She was no use to anyone, lying here like this. Least of all to Cornelius.

She sighed. Oliver's cousin had been so patient, and an ever-present support. Originally, they had planned to marry and now, with Oliver dead, there was nothing to stand in their way, she supposed. But she could feel no joy at the prospect. Too much had happened. She missed her baby so badly. She could not imagine time healing that hurt.

A knock, and here was Nurse with the tray. 'Your chocolate, Madam.'

'Thank you.' It smelled dark and rich. And if Ellen had been right and the drink was helping her to dull the deep pain, why not take it as usual?

But what else had Ellen said? That her child might be alive after all? Impossible. But she could not dismiss that chance. She sighed.

'I fear it may be a little hot as yet. If you could put it on the table, just there, please.'

'I mixed it myself, Madam. It is just as you like it.'

Madeleine yawned. 'I am sure it is. But I am so tired.' If the woman meant to stand over her as usual, the plan must fail before it had begun.

There was another knock. A maid — one of the new ones she could not recognise; there seemed so many now. The girl spoke so quickly that Madeleine could not catch what she said, but Nurse gave an exclamation, placed the cup on the bedside table and hurried out. Almost as if Ellen had arranged it. Perhaps she had.

'So I must play my part,' Madeleine murmured.

She leaned over. The gap in the

boards was indeed there. She had not dreamed that. Not easy to tip the cup into the right place, and some splashed onto the carpet. Surely someone would notice? But it was done. And the effort had tired her somewhat, but by no means as much as she might have expected. Nothing else to do now but wait and see whether Ellen came back. No doubt she would be asleep in five minutes, as usual.

But she was not. Madeleine lay there, her eyes open, surprised as time passed at how much better she was beginning to feel. No doubt the soporific in the chocolate had been kindly meant, to help her through the worst of her grief, but if what Ellen said was true — ? They must act somehow to find out. She must make shift, after speaking to Ellen again, to get out of bed and begin to manage her own affairs.

She had been such a burden on poor Cornelius; he must have been at his wits' end. Nurse had obviously exceeded her instructions. No doubt a sleeping patient was less trouble. When her strength was fully restored, Madeleine would send for Cornelius and he could dismiss the nurse. But for now she would pretend to be asleep, as Ellen had suggested.

She muttered restlessly as the nurse entered, hoping to convince, but the woman hardly glanced at her. She was seemingly more concerned about someone else who had followed her in.

Madeleine risked a glance. 'She won't give you any trouble,' the nurse said. 'She'll sleep for an hour or so now, if not more.'

It was the same maid again. 'What if she wants something to eat?'

'She won't. If I'm still out by then, Cropper will take over as usual. This being my afternoon off, well earned at that.' The door closed behind her.

Madeleine heard the maid approaching the bed. She resisted the strong temptation to open her eyes and tried to breathe normally.

'Poor lady,' the girl said. 'It don't

seem right to me. But what do I know?'

Could she trust her? Madeleine dared not take the risk, having come this far. But if Ellen did not come back, she might have to.

Why had Ellen disappeared so abruptly in the first place? There were too many unanswered questions. And she was hungry now. More so than she had known in days. But she must not eat anything brought by her supposed guardians. She needed a clear head to work out what she must do.

The door opened again and her heart leapt as she heard Ellen's voice. 'Here I am. I thought she'd never go. I'm getting sick to death of that broom cupboard, I can tell you.'

The maid seemed hesitant and unsure. 'This will be all right, won't it? I daren't lose this place.'

'You won't. Don't worry. Stand over by the door, and tell me if anyone comes near.'

No further need for pretence, surely? Madeleine pushed herself up against the pillows. 'Ellen — so it really is you. Thank goodness. I thought you were a dream. What is going on?'

'That's what I'd like to know. But we'll never find out with you lying there, filled with whatever Nurse Grim is slipping into your drinks.'

'Yes. I must get up.'

'Nancy will fetch you something to eat. Or else you'll be too weak to move far at first.'

Madeleine nodded at the sense of this while Nancy exclaimed in horror. 'What if someone sees me?'

'Best if they don't. But just say you're getting something for the mistress, that she's feeling a bit better. I don't think they're all going along with Nurse's scheme.'

Once up and dressed and with the bread, cheese and ham that Nancy had brought giving her new strength, Madeleine did indeed feel a great deal recovered. She must regain control of her life.

'I must speak to Cornelius and discuss — various matters,' she said.

'He's away.' Ellen's voice was a little too abrupt, Madeleine thought. 'Gone to visit your northern estate, I believe.'

Madeleine nodded. 'I expect he will have been appointed executor. As my husband's cousin.'

'I don't know about that. But he made a big search of all Mr Oliver's papers when he died. Looking for a will, we all thought.'

Well, that would make sense. 'In that case I will not wait for his return. I shall go and see Mr Langholm this afternoon. Without delay. Then I shall know exactly where I stand. I would have expected that Oliver would have left his affairs in order — but . . . ' She shook her head.

'But he was behaving so oddly that who can tell what he might have done?' Ellen suggested.

'Yes, I'm afraid so. When the nurse gets back, I shall be confident that I have the full authority to dismiss her.'

'And not before time,' Ellen said darkly.

2

William Franklyn paused, regarding the solidly respectable London square. This was the house, he decided. A pleasant residence, overlooking the central gardens. The street was not without the usual scattering of loungers and beggars, as so often happened — but that was all to the good. His own presence would be less remarked.

This was difficult. He wished, not for the first time, that he had not agreed to the lady's request but knew he could not have refused. She had been so distressed. Her story had been strange and not a little confused.

He hardly knew her; had only just made her acquaintance when accompanying his father to take the spa waters in the northern seaside resort of Falsborough. She was quite recently widowed, it seemed, and her husband had been a boyhood friend of William's father. One afternoon, his father had gone out and with a sense of resignation, William had begun sorting through a pile of papers his father had thrust upon him.

It was almost as if Mrs Belmont had waited for the opportunity to find him alone in their rented rooms. She was heavily veiled and clasping her hands together as she begged for his help. 'For I do not know where to turn.'

'Of course,' William had responded politely. 'If I can.'

'It was here,' she had said, weeping into a lace handkerchief. 'This is where it all began. Again, I had come for the waters — and to introduce my daughter into society. Our eldest child and very dear.'

At the Assembly, it seemed, her daughter had met someone quite unsuitable. Fortunately, the young man's cousin, older and possessing more money and property, became interested. A better arrangement in every way.

'Since my husband's death . . . ' She had covered her face with her hand. 'My circumstances have not been as I would wish. It is important that my daughters marry well.' She had been pleased to see her eldest settled so easily, she explained.

'And what did your daughter think of this alteration?' William had asked. 'Exchanging one suitor for another?'

'Oh — Madeleine did not like it at all. But in the end one does not argue with financial necessity.'

William nodded. He could well believe it. Parents must be practical when considering marriage for their daughters. He sighed. That was the way of the world, however regrettable it might seem at times.

All that had been easy to understand; the remainder less so. Perhaps because the distressed mother hardly understood it herself. The daughter became pregnant, to the joy of her husband and family. Every man needs an heir. But then, suddenly, he was making accusations that the child was not his. Whether or not these accusations were ill-founded, she did not know. For the husband had died suddenly — and apparently, the child also.

'Fortunate, then, that your daughter could have your love and support,' William said gravely.

She gave an audible sob. 'Ah, no. I dare not follow my maternal feelings. I have a prospective suitor in mind for my next daughter in age. But he is a man to whom respectability is of the utmost importance. I must refrain from all contact with Madeleine lest he is put off. It is a most difficult situation.'

'But surely you do not give credence to these accusations? Against your very dear child, as you said?'

'I do not know what to believe. But I dare not take such a risk without indisputable proof of her innocence. I wrote to her, explaining my position. And told her that I must not write again.'

William frowned. How unfeeling this suitor must be, to dismiss a prospective bride on such unjust and flimsy grounds. He felt very sorry for the widow's daughters — and the eldest, Madeleine, in particular.

* * *

Now, he came to himself as a cab rattled past noisily. While he was in London about his father's concerns, he must do whatever he was able; the sad tale wrung his heart. Hence his stance here. But he did not know what he would be able to achieve. Already he had seen the family lawyer arrive, only to be turned away. Fortunately Mr Langholm, a highly regarded lawyer with many northern clients including the Franklyn family, was already known to him. But William had less reason than he to be admitted to this house.

And now what? All he could do for the moment, it seemed, was to observe the house and see what happened.

So far, he had had little luck. A week ago, the dark young man he had decided must be the rejected suitor and younger cousin, had left with baggage and not yet returned. William had already observed that the most obvious lounger, with a narrow face and unpleasant look, had made himself scarce whenever the cousin had appeared. And now the young man's absence seemed to mean that the lounger had been in place almost constantly. Perhaps he too was watching the house? But why?

His thoughts were once again interrupted. A cab had appeared at the door. He had not noticed anyone come out to summon it; that was what came of allowing himself to become lost in thought. Still, he could make up for that now. He must not make his interest too obvious, but his senses were alert at once. The door of the house was opening. He gave a sharp intake of breath. This had to be the lady herself. Pale and drawn, but with a fragile loveliness that tore at his heart.

He strode quickly to the end of the square ready to hail a cab to follow, knowing he must not draw any attention to himself. As the vehicle passed him, however, he could not resist glancing in. The lady looked startled, as well she might. He chided himself, *You fool. You are not to fall in love with her. Her life is complicated and tragic enough*.

But he had a feeling that it was already too late.

⋆ ⋆ ⋆

Calling for the carriage would take too long, Madeleine decided. Besides, she did not yet wish to make her movements known to the servants. Not until she was certain of her position. Ellen agreed to summon a cab, assuring her that no one would see her.

Annoyingly, once outside the house, her limbs would not move as well as Madeleine had hoped. She had been too long lying inactive while events had hurried on without her. As she had to take advantage of Ellen's arm, going down the steps, she was angry and frustrated with herself. What a picture she must make — a poor, feeble invalid. She paused to gain breath and scanned the street to see who might be watching. *How foolish*, she told herself. *Who would be in the slightest bit interested in the movements of what must seem a poor sick lady?* And this had always been a pleasant, quiet street, away from the bustle of the main thoroughfare, set around the green, square gardens.

And yet, today, there were loungers taking an unwarranted interest. The nearest was a man leaning on the railings wearing a shabby coat and battered hat. He had a narrow face and a leering expression. She shivered.

'Who is that?' she asked her maid.

'Oh, don't mind him.' Ellen said briskly. 'He seems to have taken up a position here. Begging, I shouldn't wonder. When he discovers he'll gain nothing here, he will soon move on. Come, I will help you into the cab.'

Madeleine was not so sure. As the cab set off, they passed closely to where the man was standing and he made no attempt at pretence; he was blatantly regarding them. The sharp features held a knowing look that made Madeline shudder as they reached the corner.

And here she became aware that she was looking into the eyes of another stranger. A man in a dark blue, well-fitting coat. He half-smiled, putting a hand to his hat. Her eyes widened and it was all she could do to resist smiling back.

Surely she had never been introduced to this man? She would not have forgotten him easily. An open, pleasant face but with a strength she felt at once able to trust. Some unexpected warmth stirred in her breast — and this was madness! She had never met him before and he in no way resembled Cornelius, her first love, with his dark brooding looks.

And yet he, too, gave the distinct impression that he already knew her.

This was ridiculous. Here she was, intending to take up her own affairs and responsibility and indulging in girlish fancies. This would not do!

The journey to the lawyer's house did not take long. For a moment, having rung the bell, she wondered whether she should have sent a note inviting Mr Langholm to the house. But that would have only meant further delay. If the clerk who opened the door thought her behaviour odd, he hid it well. She stated in a clear voice, 'Mrs Corning to see Mr Langholm, if you please. I believe he will see me.'

He bowed slightly. 'Indeed, Madam. I will tell him immediately.' He was back in moments to gesture her through into the inner room as if he were well aware of who she was. Maybe the unusual circumstances had been the talk of the chambers. And Mr Langholm himself was emerging to greet her, his face suitably arranged to express pleasure and sorrow.

'My dear Mrs Corning, please allow me to express my condolences.'

'Thank you. I am sorry to be so late in seeking this interview. It is some time since my husband's death but I have been — indisposed.'

'Of course. Quite understandable. I am very pleased to see you recovered. But there was no need to tax your strength by making the journey here. I would have come to you — indeed, will do so whenever you wish.'

He spoke politely, but without undue warmth. That was understandable, she thought, as she had never met him before. Oliver had dealt with everything. Would he prove an ally? *But come*, she scolded herself, *I must have no need of allies. I must learn to act on my own account*.

She sat on the chair before the desk and declined refreshment. 'I will speak frankly, Mr Langholm. I need to know where I stand. I believe my husband's cousin, Mr Cornelius Corning, has been handling my affairs during my illness. As I believe he is perfectly entitled to do.'

Mr Langholm hesitated. 'Entitled?'

'As my husband's executor.'

'Ah, I understand. But I am afraid you are mistaken. Your husband did not name his cousin as executor. I believe . . . ' Mr Langholm steepled his hands. 'He may have had that intention at one point — but he never fulfilled his purpose.' He paused.

Behind her, Ellen coughed. Madeleine understood. She, too, felt there was something the lawyer was not telling her. She said, 'Oh?' But Mr Langholm was leafing through the papers on his desk.

His next words did not answer her unspoken question. 'In the terms of the will made by your husband last year, I myself was named as sole executor. I am very pleased that I am able to fulfil my duties at last. I have visited your home more than once but, of course, during your illness have been denied admittance. Your servants certainly have your best interests at heart. Their loyalty is commendable, in preserving your rest.'

Madeleine frowned a little. Commendable? 'Indeed. I am very sorry that you have had more than one fruitless journey.'

'No matter. We may proceed now.'

How fortunate that she had come here. No one had told her that the solicitor had wished to see her. She did not recall anyone attempting to rouse her. But no doubt Cornelius had ordered that she should have complete rest and quiet, thinking he was acting for the best. She became aware that Mr Langholm was waiting quietly. 'Certainly. Pray do so.'

The lawyer resumed, 'The latest will I hold was dated the fifteenth day of September, of last year — 1840.' He paused as if allowing her to make a conclusion from this.

'September the fifteenth. Oh — I

see.' She nodded, mindful of his delicacy. They had been certain by then that she was with child, and Oliver had been so proud — and happy. Yes, he had. She had surely not imagined it. It was difficult now to order events in her mind.

'This must be painful for you. Subsequent events were difficult, I know.'

'Yes.' A terrible time. She did not know how she would have survived it without the help and support of dear Cornelius.

'Therefore,' Mr Langholm continued, 'the will left everything to the child that was to be born.'

'But he — is dead.'

'So I have been informed. By Mr Cornelius. I am very sorry.' He paused. 'What were the exact circumstances, if I may so enquire? A sudden childhood illness?'

'I do not recall. I am afraid I do not know. Both tragic events and happening so closely together — I was taken ill.'

Perhaps beneath the legal façade, his expression was softening. Should they confide in him? She half-turned to Ellen, who nodded encouragement.

But Mr Langholm was speaking again. 'Of course, in the event of the child's death, everything is left to yourself. You are the sole beneficiary.'

Indeed. This was why Mr Langholm was making such a point of stating the date. That was before Oliver changed and became so unaccountably angry with her. She remembered her own voice, pleading, almost weeping, 'But Oliver, what have I done?'

And his snarling reply, 'You know that, Madam. You know very well.'

'Your husband was considering making a new will — but I have to tell you that I am glad he did not. He discussed this with me — and we made an initial draft, against my strongest advice. I should not be telling you this, but if you should discover a later will concealed about the house, I have no doubt that it will do yourself the greatest disservice. We could — and would — contest it, of course, on the grounds of your husband not being of sound mind and suffering from delusions. I asked him repeatedly if he had any grounds for his accusations, and he gave me no sensible answer.

'Legally, of course, the child was his heir. There can be no question of that.' He clasped his hands on the desk.

Was there to be any end to these riddles? No one seemed to be able to give her a straight answer. 'I do not understand. What do you mean?'

He said gently, 'I thought you knew. Your husband had come to believe that the child was not his.'

Madeleine remembered now. The dark fears and memories that she had been trying to suppress came flooding back. Once again, she felt that unbearable pain of the unjust accusation. The dark, poisonous untruths that had obsessed her husband, seemingly for no reason.

And her mother had seemed to believe them also; she recalled the devastating letter she had received, telling her to cease all contact with her family lest she damage her sisters' prospects. She put a hand to her throat, the black leather glove warm against her cold skin. 'That is not true.'

'As I thought. But there is no need to distress yourself further.'

'Yes, for I must be strong.' She heard herself adding, without considering the wisdom of this, 'I am not certain that my child is dead.'

His face became closed. The growing warmth was wiped away at a stroke. 'I expect this is understandable.'

She had made a mistake; he would think her delusional also. He was a lawyer, dealing in proven facts, not surmises. She said briskly, 'Of course. It is merely an effect of my regrettable illness and when I have discussed the matter with Cornelius and visited the church where he is buried, I will be able to accept my loss and grieve fully, I am sure.'

As she spoke, she knew even more strongly that she did not believe it. But this was what she would do. She would make her own investigations.

'My main purpose in coming to see you was to establish that I am enabled to manage my own affairs, as a widow.'

The lawyer's relief was almost laughable. 'Certainly.' They passed the next few minutes in discussing the formalities of probate and the funds available to her. She need have no concerns, he assured her. She hoped she had managed to overcome the unfortunate impression she had given him.

Madeleine took her leave politely, the lawyer conducting them to the outer door himself, assuring her of his continued service. As they descended the steps, a figure coming up stood aside for her. She thanked him and some instinct caused her to look up into his face. Blue eyes filled with laughter, although he acknowledged her solemnly enough, removing his hat to reveal fair curling hair as he bowed broad shoulders.

He seemed familiar. Where had she seen him before? Of course, on the corner as they left the house not an hour ago. She had, she realised, warmed to him then, in that briefest of glimpses. And this encounter also was less than a moment before they both passed and went on.

But that shared glance had brought a brightness to the day and she entered the cab with a lighter step. Yes, she was resolved. She would find the truth of it. She needed no allies, apart from Ellen. And she intended to arrange that her maid was restored to her rightful place. All things were possible, now that she was assured of her financial position.

But before anything else, she must discover the meaning of Ellen's words. The words that had finally inspired her to get up and fight against the wave of grief and suffering that had played into the nurse's hands. They were safe here from being overheard, enclosed in the cab.

'Ellen, please tell me; how do you know my baby is still alive? Tell me everything you know.'

Ellen hesitated before answering. 'I do not know anything. Not exactly.' Her voice was troubled.

Madeleine closed her eyes. The searing grief was as fresh as it had ever been. 'Please do not tell me you said it just to rouse me.'

'No. I would not do that. But without the need to wake you, I would have waited until I could find out something further. And yet I truly do believe it. Maybe it's some kind of instinct, but I loved him too, because he was yours. You know you have always been almost like a sister to me, since we were brought up so closely together. And I feel it in my heart.'

Madeleine said sadly, 'Is that all? I understand and cannot blame you. I wish I could feel it too — but my senses have been dulled for so long.'

'No — it is more than that. A dozen small things that don't add up. Mr Oliver instructed me to take the child and have it baptised — but on no account to give a name to the father. He said, 'The child is innocent; he cannot be made to suffer for the sins of others.'

'I agreed and said I thought this was wise. But as I was getting little George ready, he came back in a different mood, having changed his mind, saying, 'I know what would happen — you would give my name and it would be false, would it not? For I am sure you must know the truth of it.' Ranting on in one of his furies and making no sense.'

'So my son was never baptised. But then — ' Madeleine's voice broke. 'Was there a burial?'

Ellen shook her head. 'I cannot say. Everything happened at once. Suddenly the cradle was empty and I went to Mr Oliver and demanded to know where he was. I thought perhaps he must have been taken ill while I was asleep, or caring for you. He said the child had gone to a relative in the country, 'Out of my sight for I cannot bear to look at him.'

'But he would not say where — and it was then that he grunted and clutched at his chest and throat and collapsed. We struggled to take him to his bed, but he died a few hours later. His heart couldn't stand the strain of all that groundless anger, if you ask me.'

She must not collapse herself, although at that moment Madeleine dearly wished she might. She had to be strong.

'But Ellen, if my husband had dismissed you, surely there was then no need for you to go?'

Ellen stared at her. 'Goodness, no, Miss Madeleine. It was not Mr Oliver who dismissed me. If that had been so, I would have made myself scarce until he had changed his mind or forgotten — and then returned.'

'Then, who? I do not understand.'

Ellen said darkly, 'It was Mr Cornelius.'

3

Madeleine felt as if she had been dealt a physical blow. 'But why?' she gasped. 'What reason did he have?'

Ellen shrugged. 'It was a difficult time for the whole household. Accusations flying everywhere. No one knowing what to believe. I supposed that Mr Cornelius was at his wit's end as to what to do for the best.'

It did make a little sense. 'Well, it is most fortunate that you came back and that I am able to put things right. I know Cornelius will be pleased that I am taking the household under control, as I ought. I shall begin by arranging your reinstatement. And the nurse's dismissal. Can you start at once?'

Ellen's joy was evident. 'I certainly can. If I may just run and tell my sister where I'll be — I've been lodging with her.'

'Mary? She lives nearby?' She remembered at once; Mary had worked for them too, but had left to marry. 'How is she?'

'Very well. She told Fred she wouldn't go far from me — and you don't have to go far from this square to find a cheaper kind of housing. And even worse. But Mary and Fred and their little one are renting a respectable cottage and are very happy.'

'Their little one? Of course. How much I've missed. And Mary will miss you when you move back here; you must have been a great help to her.'

'She knows what I wanted and will be very pleased for me. And for you.'

'Please give her my best wishes.' Mary had come here with Ellen to support Madeleine in her new life — and then found happiness with Fred, one of Oliver's grooms. So Mary was also part of her past.

But she must not dwell on that. She must face up to the problems of the present and deal with them in turn.

The housekeeper had always seemed an aloof and awe-inspiring figure to the new young bride. But now things must change. Madeleine told herself firmly, *Be afraid if you like but do not on any account show it*. Otherwise, she would never gain the status in the household that was rightfully hers.

She kept her chin high as the housekeeper entered and held her hands together in her lap to prevent them shaking. She must speak slowly and clearly. The woman's face was expressionless as she loomed above her.

'I am sorry, Mrs Burrows, that the household has been — er — rudderless for so long. Without a mistress in anything but name. But now, as you see, I am fully recovered.'

'I am very pleased to hear that, Madam.'

'I am in no way intending to undermine your authority, Mrs Burrows. I have always been very pleased with your methods and the way the household has run smoothly under your control.'

Mrs Burrows nodded, smiling a little. 'Thank you, Madam.'

'I am to make some changes, however. I am no longer in need of a nurse, as you see. And Ellen is to be reinstated as my maid.' She took a silent breath, waiting for the disapproval.

But the housekeeper nodded again. 'An excellent choice, if I may say so. It was not with my agreement that Ellen was dismissed. I would like you to know that. She had always been most satisfactory. Shall I speak to Nurse Herries on her return?'

'Oh, certainly. If you would.' Madeleine realised she had not even known the woman's name.

'And I presume I am to speak to yourself, daily from now on? Instead of to Mr Cornelius?'

'Of course.' Goodness . . . Madeleine was surprised that Cornelius had troubled himself with household matters. Yet another instance of the burden she had placed upon him — and another reason for gratitude.

'Nurse Herries may have a fair reference. And although I am dispensing with her services at once, she is to have a week's pay in lieu of notice.' She paused. 'Do you think that will be sufficient?'

'I am sure Nurse Herries will be very satisfied with that, Madam.' There was a warmth in the housekeeper's eyes. Madeleine was certain she was not imagining it. 'I am very pleased to see that you are restored to health. The household will benefit from being back to a more normal situation.' Now her approval was marked.

Madeleine was gaining the impression that Mrs Burrows had disliked the nurse too. 'Good. I think that is all.' She bowed her head, graciously.

As Mrs Burrows went out, she sank back in her chair, almost laughing with relief. How easy that had been. Cornelius would certainly be surprised on his return. She had intended asking Mrs Burrows to dismiss the nurse, but the housekeeper had been ahead of her. She was sure they would work together very well. Behind that frosty exterior, Mrs Burrows was alert and perceptive — and, if she were not mistaken, had a kind heart.

Oh — how strange. What about Ellen? Mrs Burrows had not asked whether she should contact her. Madeleine smiled. Perhaps Mrs Burrows knew more than she revealed and was well aware of Ellen's illicit visits. That would make sense, as in any well-run household it was highly unlikely that someone would be able to conceal themselves as easily as Ellen had done.

What did the housekeeper know of her baby's supposed death? Should she confide in her? No, not yet. At a later time, maybe. She must still be cautious. Until she, with Ellen's help, had discovered what had happened to him, she must take care where she gave her trust. Tomorrow, they would begin their search.

* * *

On the following morning, however, as Madeleine was making ready to leave the house — carefully letting it be known that she would be taking a walk to enable her to regain her strength — there was the flurry of an arrival.

Nancy knocked and came in as Ellen was setting the finishing touches to Madeleine's plain black dress.

'Mr Cornelius is returned, Madam. He is in the drawing room.'

'Oh!' This was earlier than she had expected. She had hoped for more time to make her enquiries and establish her new role in the household. And why was she feeling like this? She should be joyful at the prospect of seeing him again, with all that had passed between them as they fell in love.

But that had been so long ago. She had thought her heart was broken when she was made to marry Oliver, but it had carried on beating. It would only break now if she were to find that her child was not alive after all.

Her thoughts were in a turmoil as she entered the drawing room. And there he was, as darkly handsome as ever. She waited for her heart to give its customary jolt — but nothing happened. *I have suffered too much*, she thought. *That girl I was, has gone, maybe for ever*.

'Madeleine!' Cornelius strode forwards, hands outstretched. 'What a welcome surprise. When the servants said you were up, I could hardly believe it. Though you must be careful not to overtire yourself.'

His expression was so concerned that for a few moments, she weakened. He was taking her arm, guiding her to a chair near the fire. How pleasant it would be to sit back and allow someone else to care for her, and to solve all her problems.

No. She straightened her back,

smiling to soften the words. 'I am no longer an invalid. I have indulged myself too long in weakness. It is time I regained control of myself — and my life.'

Cornelius laughed. 'My dear girl, what is this? I am here to look after everything for you.'

'Not until — ' Madeleine stopped. She had been about to say, 'Not until we are married.' But saying that would commit herself to that outcome which she was no longer certain she wanted. If she were to marry Cornelius, would she ever discover the truth? If she found out anything he deemed unpleasant, he might seek to protect her. And she had to know.

No matter, because Cornelius cheerfully completed her statement. 'Not until you are my wife. As always, you show true delicacy, which is nothing less than I would expect. And it cannot be soon enough for me. You know how long I have waited for you.'

'We cannot rush into anything.

Society would condemn us — and rightly.'

He pursed his lips. 'Of course. We are constrained by convention. And we must therefore wait. But the waiting will be all the sweeter with our end at last in sight.' He moved swiftly towards her and she knew that in a moment she would be within his arms. She slid adroitly from her chair and moved towards the door.

'No, Cornelius. I am sorry but it is too soon.'

He frowned. 'I respected your wish, as a wife, to remain faithful even though your husband was none of your choosing. But you cannot now play the grieving widow, surely? You are not going to tell me you loved my cousin Oliver? We both know that you did not. Added to which, his treatment of you latterly surely negated any misplaced sense of loyalty you may have had.'

'Yes, I know. I may not grieve for him unduly, although he was kind to me at first. But, Cornelius . . . ' She took a deep breath. 'I do grieve for my child.'

'Your child?' His surprise seemed genuine. 'Oliver's child? But its life was so short. I thought you would have forgotten it; the child of a man you never loved.' He smiled confidently. 'You will have other children. Yours and mine. They are the ones who will matter to you.'

She stared at him in horror. 'You do not understand.'

'Maybe it is different for women, fair, frail creatures that you are. So tender-hearted. But if you have not forgot yet, then trust me, you soon will.'

Madeleine answered with quiet intensity. 'I shall never forget him.'

He shrugged. 'Well, we shall not argue about it. You see, you are not as strong, emotionally, as you thought. But that is why I am here. To take all burdens from those beautiful shoulders while you rest and recover.'

He seemed about to caress her beautiful shoulders; she moved again.

'Who has been handling my affairs

during my illness?'

'I have, naturally. My cousin named me as his executor and I have taken everything into my own hands. On your behalf, of course. I was accustomed to working with Oliver upon his business interests and with the northern estate. That was why I had to absent myself — but if I had known that you would make such an unexpected recovery, and so soon, I would never have left at such a time.'

'And household matters?'

'I am sorry?' He seemed perplexed as he shook his head.

'Some of my servants had been dismissed. I admit, for many weeks I did not know what was happening around me but when I recovered my senses . . . Well, it was confusing to discover unfamiliar faces tending to me.'

He was still shaking his head. 'I am not certain what you mean.'

'Ellen? My personal maidservant? Whom I knew from childhood and came with me from home?'

'Ah — Ellen. Yes, I believe she was not suitable.'

'In what way?'

'I do not know the details. Why would I? You know how your husband was before he died. Or maybe you do not remember? That time will be obscured by your illness.' He looked at her keenly.

'I remember some of it,' Madeleine said slowly. 'And wish I did not.'

'Yes. He became very confused, making accusations that were often quite unfounded.' He hesitated. 'I do not wish to bring you further pain if you have forgotten, but you yourself were at the centre of his illusions.'

'I believe so.' Mr Langholm had intimated as much. Should she tell Cornelius about her visit to the solicitor? And of course she should. Why was she holding back on this? Perhaps during her time of pain and torment she had lost the ability to trust, even the most proven and loyal people.

But the moment had passed. He was continuing, 'Oliver was convinced, in his disordered mind, that the child was not his. That explains of course his inability to accept the child and his regrettable rejection of you.'

'I gave him no cause for such a belief.'

He gave a short laugh. 'No, you did not. And none better than I to know that. Your conduct throughout your brief marriage was strictly honourable. And I admire you greatly for it — although I could not like it. But now there is surely no longer any need.' And before she could avoid him once more, his arms were round her and he was kissing her.

At first, she tried to push him away but then suddenly she was once more a girl of seventeen, meeting a handsome stranger at the Assembly in Falsborough. She had been swept away by his embraces, the slight roughness of his face against hers and the strength of his enfolding arms. She had been so happy;

she had been exalted with joy. Their romance had progressed with all the conventions observed as she had been introduced to his relatives and he to hers. She could not believe her happiness. Until Cornelius approached her mother to seek her approval, only to be told that his finances were not sufficient and that the young man's own cousin, Oliver Corning, being interested, Madeleine was to be given to him instead. An older, wealthier man — more suitable in every way.

The recollections passed through her mind in less than a moment. If she had wondered whether his kisses would reawaken those long-ago feelings, now she knew that they would not. That girl was gone, her love numbed with grief and pain. If only she could find her child, or at the very least discover what had happened to him, maybe they would return. She did not know.

He must have sensed her lack of response, for his grasp loosened and she was able to push him away. 'No. I am sorry. I told you, it is too soon.'

'You are right. Maybe the convention of waiting for a year before we marry is a wise one. But by then you will have recovered, I am certain of that. And, see, I am as aware of appearances as you are. I will not stay under your roof. That was acceptable when Oliver was alive and I worked for him, and also when you were ill. But not now, I am afraid. I shall seek lodgings.'

She was surprised. No doubt he was bluffing and had expected her to regard that prospect with dismay. She made a small hopeless gesture with her hands which could have meant anything. She was not certain herself.

Choosing her words carefully, she said, 'Considering all that has passed between us and what may come about in the future, I believe it would be wise for you to live elsewhere. I do feel we should regard the conventions.'

She could see that he was disconcerted, although he concealed it well. She had been right. He had not expected her to agree so easily.

'Your reputation and conventions are all-important, my love. But I shall make sure I am near at hand to continue to manage everything for you.'

Now she was upon firmer ground. She smiled. 'I very much appreciate all that you have done for me. But I am able to manage my own affairs now.'

He stared at her. 'What? But how can you — a mere child, innocent of the ways of the world?'

'I am a woman now, Cornelius. It is high time I took responsibility for myself.' She smiled, thinking how pleased and surprised he would be. 'I have already made a beginning, in your absence. Yesterday evening, I made myself familiar with all the papers in Oliver's desk. I must know what needs to be done.'

He did not seem pleased. 'This is most unwise — in your state of health. You will become ill again.'

'I am coming to that. Regarding my illness, I am afraid I have had to let

Nurse Herries go. No doubt she was necessary when she was appointed, when I was suffering from shock and an excess of grief, I believe — but now she is no longer needed.'

He said stiffly, 'All this is far too soon. I cannot agree.'

'She was interpreting her instructions too fiercely,' Madeleine insisted. 'Indeed, she was sedating me when there was no longer cause. However, I am sure it did me good — for see how strong I feel now. I am completely recovered.'

He said only, 'You must take care.' He paused, tapping one hand upon the other. 'Did you find any recent papers in your searches? Anything with Oliver's signature made in the last weeks before he died?'

'Ah, you mean a new will.' She was pleased to demonstrate to him how quickly she had grasped his meaning. 'There was no sign of anything like that. And I have been to see Mr Langholm and discussed the situation with him. See how organised I have become.'

'You have been to see Mr Langholm?'

'That seemed the best way to begin. I knew you would be surprised. And pleased.' Her voice was becoming defiant.

He bowed slightly. 'Certainly. You have been very busy, and in a short space of time. I am amazed.'

'If I do this now, I shall be more useful to you later. As helpmeet and partner in business affairs.'

'There is no need.'

'It is what I wish,' she said gently. 'Anyhow, we must not quarrel over it. There is something else we must talk about.' Her breath caught in her throat. There was a leaden feeling around her heart.

'Yes?' He looked expectant.

'My child. I wish . . . I wish I could have attended his burial.'

His eyes seemed wary. 'You were too ill. Such an occasion would have distressed you far too much.'

'I accept that. But I wish to visit his grave. Where is it?'

'There is no headstone,' Cornelius answered hastily. 'Such things take time. And I am not sure whether such a visit would be wise. Yes,' as she was opening her mouth in firm protest, 'I see you are determined upon it. I will arrange to escort you myself.'

'Thank you. The burial will have taken place at St Michael's? Rather than St John's?'

'Oh, St Michael's. Yes. Certainly.'

She did not doubt that he would regret that admission on giving it some thought. Better to change the subject altogether. 'But I am remiss. I have not asked you about your visit — and all on my behalf it seems. So how were the estates at Brierley?'

He said stiffly, 'Shall I make a report to you? I can do so if you wish, everything itemised and catalogued.'

'No, of course not. A simple affirmative will suffice.'

He smiled. 'Then yes. There is nothing for you to worry about at Brierley.'

'That is good to hear. Thank you.'

'So — I will make my new arrangements forthwith, and see that my rooms here are cleared.' Cornelius prepared to take his leave.

'The servants will assist you in anything you need.' She hesitated. There was something else she had not asked.

'When Oliver was confused — I need to be clear about this — was it he who dismissed Ellen and appointed Nurse Herries?'

He shrugged, his hand already reaching for the door. 'Yes, of course it was. Who else?'

4

Madeleine stared after Cornelius as the door closed behind him. That was not what Ellen had said. He was lying. But why? Unless Ellen was lying — and she had never known her maid to do so. But time was passing. She must set out on her all-important quest and discover the truth. Hopefully if she slipped out now, with Ellen, Cornelius would be taken up with making new arrangements for his accommodation and would not notice. But her story would remain the same, whoever might ask. She was taking the air for the benefit of her health.

Arriving on foot and dressed plainly in black as they both were, it was hardly surprising that the vicar did not seem to welcome her request.

'I do not recall the burial of every child,' he said. 'There are so many.'

'There will surely be records kept?'

The vicar sighed resignedly. 'Indeed. I suppose you will need to consult the registers.'

'If you please. And if there should be a charge for this service, I am most willing to pay it.'

'Very well. No, there will be no charge. As it happens, there has been another enquiry this morning, so I will be avoiding the trouble of getting them out afresh. This way, if you please.' He led the way into the vestry, where someone else was studying the books spread upon a table. 'Ah, Mr Franklyn, you have not yet finished?'

There was that same warm shock as he turned, smiling. But this time, she had more opportunity to study his face.

'Indeed I have, thank you. My father is insistent that I must make certain of the exact date. Much depends on it. But I have it now.' He bowed, smiling at Madeleine directly. 'Good morning, ladies. William Franklyn.'

She found herself responding. 'Mrs

Oliver Corning.' Although this was hardly appropriate as an introduction, she thought. 'I believe we have already met, at Mr Langholm's office.'

'We did.' He bowed again. 'I will leave you to your enquiries.'

'Thank you.' Her heart was thudding. Even so, she managed a wry smile as she saw the vicar, while ushering him out, discreetly but swiftly accepting payment. Of course. This was how things were done — and if that was needful, she would take care to do the same.

'How odd that we should see him again so soon,' she murmured to Ellen.

The vicar returned, his manner suddenly much warmer. 'Mrs Oliver Corning? But of course, we buried your husband quite recently. I am so sorry for your loss. I did not recognise you. You must be distraught.'

'Yes, indeed. I regret that I was not able to attend the service. I was ill.'

'Understandable.' He nodded solemnly. No sign now of the mild irritation at the interruption to his busy schedule. 'How may I assist you?'

She swallowed. 'For now, my thoughts are with my child. Our child. I was insensible with grief, it seems, and could not attend to our baby son as I ought. A great deal passed without my knowledge. Reverend Linguard — I would now, belatedly, like to see his grave.'

'You mean, your husband's grave? There is no stone arranged as yet but I can show you the plot.'

'No — though, of course, I should like to see that too. But I wish to know where my child is buried.'

The vicar hesitated.

'Of course,' Madeleine said. 'How foolish of me. They will be sharing the same grave.'

The cleric responded in a low voice, 'I was not aware that the child had died. I am sorry.' After an awkward pause, he continued. 'When did this sad occurrence take place? Let me check.' He was turning pages. 'There are several babies listed here — but all are known to me. There was no one else from Mr Corning's family — or address.'

Madeleine was quivering, hardly daring to hope. The vicar offered his arm and escorted her outside, to the newly dug earth that held Oliver. She was in a daze, hardly able to respond. She stared at the unmarked ground, feeling nothing except an urgent need to begin her search. As now she must, in earnest. The vicar's condolences seemed to go on for ever, and she must nod and smile her thanks. 'But we have taken up too much of your time already. As you said, you have other, pressing duties.'

'My dear Madam, what could be more pressing than offering comfort to the bereaved? No, no.' But at last he took his leave.

Madeleine could hardly wait until he was beyond hearing. 'Oh, Ellen, you were right. My child may well be alive.'

'We can only hope so. But we have

only proved he is not buried here.'

'But why would he be anywhere else? And Cornelius *said* he was here.'

'So he did.' Ellen's voice was dry.

'Oh, Ellen, I cannot blame you for holding a grudge against Cornelius when he dismissed you — although I am sure he thought he was acting for the best.' Why was she supporting him in this way? Maybe because she felt guilty at no longer returning his love. And yet she also had a duty to Ellen.

She said firmly, 'That will certainly not occur again. Your place is here with me, and is assured. I need you. No, I will face Cornelius with our discovery and ask for the truth.'

'Is that wise? If he lied once, he may do so again. Though, no doubt, that too was all for the best.'

'Why should he? When I convince him that I am strong enough to bear the truth, whatever it is. And if little George is not dead — where is he? I must find him.' She twisted her hands together. She must not weep.

Ellen pressed her arm. 'Yes, of course. Do not upset yourself. But how?'

A deep voice said, 'May I be of any assistance?'

Madeleine knew who it would be before she turned. A mixture of emotions swept through her. Wanting to accept his help while knowing she should not, and feeling an unsuitable pleasure in his presence, she found herself blushing. 'Well — I am sorry — a kind offer I am sure. But I do not know you.' She thought impatiently, *Why do I need to bow to these conventions? And I am a widow now. The rules are different.*

Mr Franklyn smiled. 'It could be said that the Reverend Linguard all but introduced us, not half an hour ago. And we have a mutual acquaintance in Mr Langholm. I know he would vouch for me if required. But I took the liberty of approaching you because I can see that you are distressed. If it is something arising from the Registers, I may well be able to help. I have gained experience through unravelling a matter within my own family — at my father's bidding.'

Her voice was still shaking. 'And you were successful?'

'Indeed I was. And am in a position to bring the problem to the only fair conclusion. Although I doubt that my father will be altogether pleased with the result.' He smiled. 'But he will come round, I am sure.'

She was hardly aware of what he was saying as the warm, deep voice washed over her. Maybe he was giving her time to compose herself. That was a thoughtful gesture, if so. She warmed to him even more. How could she then dismiss him politely and hurry away?

She found herself saying, 'Your offer could be most opportune. Thank you.' She glanced at Ellen, expecting a look of disapproval, but Ellen was smiling, too. What was it about him that even the sensible Ellen could be so easily won over? But come — she must behave in a businesslike way, to make the most of his help.

Was he a gentleman? He was well spoken and well-dressed but not, as far as she could judge, with excessive expense. She was not certain how to proceed, but she knew she must not offend him.

Madeleine said carefully, 'Forgive me, but are you offering your services in a professional capacity? I only ask — ' She hesitated. 'I have been looking to employ someone in my search. I would be more than willing to pay such a person a fair price. As a widow, I do not have the male assistance other ladies might expect. I would not know where to begin, to find someone.'

He nodded. 'It would not be easy, to find someone you could trust. Payment is not necessary; I would just like to help. But then, if a professional basis would be more acceptable to you, I have no objection. If you wish, the financial arrangements could be made through Mr Langholm.'

'Yes indeed.' Surely nothing could be more respectable?

He pointed to a seat in the shade of a yew tree. 'If we sit here a moment, you can tell me what is troubling you. Unless you would prefer me, perhaps, to call at your home?'

Madeleine thought quickly. He might encounter Cornelius; would that be a good idea? She was determined to find her child without Cornelius. And the less he knew about it the better, with his misplaced notions of what might be best for her. She said decisively, 'That would only delay matters. I need to begin my search as soon as possible.'

They sat down and she made her account brisk and businesslike. Otherwise she might not be able to prevent the tears. But she avoided mentioning Oliver's strange suspicions. How would that assist anything?

Mr Franklyn impressed her immediately with his swift grasp of her situation. 'It does seem to me that we have grounds for some hope.'

'You do not think me merely a hysterical female, clutching at straws?'

'Indeed not. Although if you were, that would be understandable.'

'So, Mr Franklyn — ' Her voice wavered. 'Who has stolen my child?'

'Maybe discovering who was responsible is not of great value at this point,' he said slowly. 'It may well have been your husband, if his behaviour was so erratic. But my priority is to find your son.'

'You can do that?' Her heart fluttered with hope.

He said earnestly, 'I will do my utmost. You will not regret this, I can assure you. From now on, you may leave everything to me.'

'No. Thank you, but I need to be involved in your search, at all times,' Madeleine returned firmly. 'I need to know everything you discover, and even if there is nothing. And if there is anything I can do myself, I will do it. So how do you intend to begin?'

He laughed. 'Very well, I agree. I suspect there would be no point in my disagreeing, for you would only set out to search on your own. Better by far if we work together. So. During my previous investigation, I made a great many useful contacts in the darker classes of society. I believe I shall begin with them. And I shall put the word about — if I may — that useful information will be rewarded. If that is agreeable to you?'

'Oh, indeed. Please spare no expense.'

'I shall not be too liberal with your resources. It would not do for any informants to know that you will pay any amount. And if you were to accompany me at this stage, it would give the impression of desperation, I feel. I shall set this in train and report back to you.'

'Yes, please.' That made sense, she supposed. 'At Mr Langholm's office. Will tomorrow be too soon?'

He paused. 'Maybe. A little. Could we say the day after? And then, I promise you, we will discuss what is to be done next.' He leaned forwards, his blue eyes filled with sympathy. 'I know you will be afire with impatience. There is so much at stake for you.'

In that moment, she felt that she would trust him with her life. She nodded gratefully. 'Thank you, yes.'

'May I escort you home?'

'No — I thank you.' Cornelius would in all likelihood be about, still making his arrangements to leave. 'I will sit here, in this fleeting sunshine, and collect my thoughts. And it is but a short walk, which will do me good.'

He touched his hat and they watched him striding away, through the church-yard gate and out into the noise of the street.

* * *

It was as if, Madeleine thought, those keen eyes had placed her under a spell. As soon as the mesmerism of his gaze had gone, doubts swept in. Had she really entrusted the safety of her son to a stranger, while feeling that she could not do so to Cornelius, whom she had known for so long?

She said, 'What do you think, Ellen?'

Ellen, usually so forthright, paused. 'He is very plausible and very pleasing to look upon. He had us both enthralled, I must admit. But paying him through Mr Langholm was a wise precaution — and insisting on no reward to be passed on until you see the results for yourself. Time will tell.'

'He seemed wholly respectable. And well-spoken.'

'Smartly but sombrely dressed, with nothing of the dandy about him. A gentleman down on his luck, I would say, if he needs to seek employment. Why else would he approach you? But don't look downcast; he may well be sincere, and who else do we have? We'll keep an eye on him.'

In the distance, Madeleine could still see Mr Franklyn, through the railings. There was no mistaking his blue coat.

As he reached the corner, he paused — as if speaking to someone. She stood up quickly. 'Come, Ellen.'

They hurried to the gate. There were only the ordinary passers-by to be seen: a woman with a bundle of washing, another woman with two children, two smart young men about town and a man with a black coat and slouch hat leaning against the wall. His arms were folded and his eyes closed. No sign of Mr Franklyn.

Ellen observed, 'That man's there again. The one who was outside the house as we left.'

Madeleine felt a chill crawl down her spine. She tried to keep her voice calm. 'I thought so. I noticed him too.'

'He was outside Mr Langholm's as well.'

That was when Madeleine had been distracted by blue eyes and broad shoulders. 'Oh!' The man was standing just where Mr Franklyn had paused. 'Did you — ?' Her voice failed her. She tried again. 'Mr Franklyn stopped just there. Did you see him? Did he speak to that man?'

She and Ellen exchanged worried glances. Ellen said, 'We must not be too hasty. After all, Mr Franklyn told us he would begin by asking around. That man looks just the sort who might be roped in to give information.'

'Yes, of course. That would explain it.' Madeleine's heart sang with relief. 'I am being foolish. We must remain clear and calm; else how may we assess anything Mr Franklyn discovers?'

Still, the repeated sightings of the man seemed more than coincidence.

'Maybe . . . ' she murmured.

'We could ask him,' Ellen said.

'Who? Mr Franklyn?'

'No, that man in the black hat. Or I could. Not you, of course.'

Madeleine was sorely tempted. She hated this uncertainty. She ached to have real knowledge of what was happening. She said reluctantly, 'Would we not frighten him off? We might spoil everything.'

Ellen sighed. 'Yes, you're right. And see — he's gone. Perhaps he knew we were talking about him.'

'Or perhaps he has hurried off to earn the reward Mr Franklyn has promised him.'

Ellen shrugged. 'That may be true.'

'We will be alert and aware,' Madeleine said. 'At all times.' *And hope and pray that Mr Franklyn would prove successful*, she added silently.

5

Unable to sleep, Madeleine was up early for what promised to be merely a day of waiting. But she had hardly finished her breakfast when Ellen came to bring a welcome diversion.

'I need to show you something that Sally found in Mr Cornelius' old room, when she was cleaning this morning.'

Madeleine could see that she was holding a paper of some kind. 'Not a new will?' Her heart stood still.

'No, no,' Ellen reassured her quickly. 'It's a page of a newspaper. Sally can't read, of course, but it's lucky that you taught me when we were children. See, it is a page from the Falsborough Gazette. And Mr Cornelius has marked this advertisement.'

Madeleine took it and read it quickly. 'I don't see — ah! Nurse Herries.'

'Advertising her services. The paper

had fallen behind a cupboard. I don't suppose Mr Cornelius meant to leave it.'

'There are plenty of suitable nurses in London, I would have thought — '

There was a knock at the door and a servant came to announce that a Mr William Franklyn had left a note. Madeleine was trembling as she opened it, reading it quickly. 'Oh! I will come at once. Ellen, he has news. We are to meet him in the churchyard.'

'But that was not the arrangement.'

'Never mind that. I need my drab cloak, quickly. We are to meet someone there. See, he says he has given no money as yet but requires me to be there for identification.'

'You mean, he has found him? Already?'

'I think that must be what has happened. Oh, Ellen, I am all fingers and thumbs. Hurry, please. This person, whoever it is, may not stay.'

'If money has been promised, they'll be in no hurry. Why don't you let me go? I know little George as well as you.'

Better, as it happened. They both knew that. But there was nothing on earth that would keep Madeleine from this meeting. 'What kind of a mother was I?' she fretted. 'I failed him, badly. I will not neglect him now.'

'No one would ever think that. And, Miss Madeleine — be sure to ask to see the birthmark on his left foot.'

'Birthmark?' She could have wept. She had not even known of it. Her knowledge of her son had been so brief. 'Thank you, Ellen. I am lucky to have you with me.' As they turned the corner and left the square, William Franklyn came away from the churchyard gates to meet them. He was alone.

'He has not left? We came as quickly as we could.' Madeleine looked past him eagerly. The churchyard seemed empty; no sign of that familiar figure who had tracked their movements so closely over the past days.

'He is behind the yew. Not wishing to make his presence known.'

She felt shaky with relief. 'My child — he has a birthmark. On his left foot.'

He nodded approval. 'That is excellent. Just the kind of evidence we need. But do not tell him exactly what we are looking for.'

She did not understand the need for that, but hardly cared. She was on fire with impatience. As they crossed the grass, however, it was not the man she expected to see who left the shadow of the yew tree but someone else, in a battered hat and greasy coat. That did not matter. She only cared about what he held in his arms — a roughly-wrapped bundle.

'Here you are, guv. I've brought him, as agreed. And will hand him over to you upon the payment of three guineas. Sterling.'

Madeleine's face was hot with longing. She made to run forward, aching to clasp the child to her breast, but William's hand restrained her. He said, 'Uncover the child first, if you please.'

'He's been well kept. He's not been injured.'

'We must ensure this is the right one.'

Madeleine was certain that it must be. She could see a fluff of dark hair beneath the dingy shawl. Her son! She knew it. Why were they wasting so much time? She stepped forward and pulled the ragged wrappings aside. The child moved its head fretfully and gave a thin, whining cry as the cold air touched him. His skin was almost the colour of his rags and he was pitifully thin. Gently, she moved the stick-like legs — and gasped in disbelief. Her hand went to her mouth, to prevent herself crying out in denial.

William Franklyn said briskly, 'This is not the right child. You have not followed my instructions.'

'I did the best I could. It's the right age. And what am I to do with it now? I've brought it all this way for nothing.'

'You'll have to take it back,' William said.

Madeleine stared at the child. So thin

and unhappy. He could so easily have been hers. The man glanced at her sharply. 'It's not wanted. Not theirs, and no room for it. That's why I thought it might be yours. They only took it in out of pity. And they'll not welcome it back with five mouths of their own to feed. But I'll have to see what I can do.' He shrugged and took the child up onto his shoulder, like a bag of rubbish.

'Wait, please.' Madeleine turned an imploring look on William. 'Could we not take him anyway? What kind of life will he have?'

William said gently, 'But he is not yours.'

'I know. But surely something can be done for him?'

Ellen said suddenly, 'I am sure my sister would take him.'

'And I could pay for his keep. I would not see her lose by it. If you are certain of this, Ellen.'

'Hey, what about my loss?' the man whined. 'I've come all this way. I was promised payment. Not to mention the kindly couple who took him in.'

'They did not want him, you said,' William returned sharply.

'Oh, pay him, please,' Madeleine urged. 'I don't want any trouble.'

William nodded. 'If you are instructing me to do so. I am acting for you.' He turned to the man. 'But let this be an end to it. You will bring no more infants that you have plucked from any poor woman of your acquaintance with too many children.'

The man touched his hat mockingly and in a single movement, took and bit the coins William proffered and thrust the baby at Ellen. And was gone, with more speed than his appearance would suggest him capable of.

Ellen said, 'Poor child. I will deliver him to Mary straight away, shall I?'

'Your mistress has too soft a heart,' William remarked. He smiled. 'And so do you. I would have thought you made of sterner stuff, Ellen. You seem a girl of great common sense.'

Ellen's voice was gruff. 'Sometimes common sense has no part. Not in the face of such need.'

William sighed. 'I know. But there are children of equal need, and worse, all over London. Please do not think you can find a home for every foundling brought to us.' He saw the mutinous look crossing Madeleine's face. 'I am sure you would if you could. And so might I. But it is hardly practical.'

Madeleine sighed. 'No, of course it is not. I am not being sensible. I know that. I have so much love waiting for my child. I did not realise my concern would extend to others; not until I saw this poor little soul.'

'My fault in part,' William confessed. 'In spreading my net so wide, I have obviously been too successful. I will interview any other applicants on my own and only consult you when I am certain I have the right one. Now I know of the birthmark, I can act alone in that respect.'

'But at least we have had a response,'

Madeleine countered. 'Your request has been taken seriously. That can only be good.'

'Indeed. The word is spreading. Our success, so quickly, took me by surprise. But I will not be caught out again. I would not cause you needless distress. Not for anything.'

They walked out of the churchyard together. Madeleine's thoughts were whirling. What had she done? What was she doing? Now she had changed the life of a poor child from the streets. Nothing would be as it would have been. *Poor child*, she thought again, stretching out to stroke the pale face.

None of them noticed the bystander in the shadows until he spoke.

'I know what you want, matey. I've found it.'

She stopped, her throat constricting. A bubble of hope rising once more, against all reason. Would it always be like this? How could she bear it?

William said quietly, 'Go with Ellen and see to your new charge, Mrs

Corning. I will deal with this. Rest assured, he will not escape me if he has sound knowledge. But I fear that our last encounter is known now — may even have been witnessed. We must not allow the news to spread that we are gullible fools.'

Madeleine sighed. 'No, I suppose not.'

'Trust me, please.' For one long moment, his face was close to hers as he strove not to be overheard. 'I do understand the depth of your feelings.'

Madeleine could hardly breathe before he smiled and moved away.

'Come, Miss Madeleine.' Ellen's hand was on her arm. 'He's right. We must see to this baby before we gain any more.' Her voice was dry.

In spite of everything, Madeleine managed a smile. 'Yes, of course. And we have yet to persuade your sister. Oh, Ellen, what if she does not want to care for someone else's child?'

They were not halfway through their tale, however, before Mary Dixon was holding out her arms. 'The poor, starved mite. Give him to me.'

'I am afraid he is none too clean,' Madeleine murmured.

'No, indeed. But that can soon be remedied. He will be washed and fed, straight away. He will be a playmate and companion for our little Edward. I will care for him as my own.'

'I will pay for his keep,' Madeleine assured her.

'I would have him anyway. But it will be sound sense to accept — and better for him. Thank you. There, there,' she crooned as the child gave another fretful cry. 'What is his name?'

'Oh — we don't know! I never thought to ask.'

'May I name him, then? Henry, perhaps.' She laughed. 'Yes, he has the look of a Henry, I think.'

They left Mary tending to little Henry and walked briskly away, Madeleine brushing away the tears, moved by Mary's welcome to a complete stranger.

'That has turned out for the best — for both of them. Little Henry is lucky. But Mr Franklyn is right. We cannot do that again. I will be much more sensible next time.'

'Leave it to Mr Franklyn, as he advised,' agreed Ellen. 'But just in case — we will borrow some clothes from Mary. If we should need to go again with Mr Franklyn to talk with such people, you will be more suitably dressed.'

'Oh, yes. Thank you.' The thought came, unbidden, that she would welcome any opportunity to meet William Franklyn. When would she see him again? But she must be patient. He would need time.

* * *

The following morning, however, Ellen had gone back to Mary's to see how the child did while Madeleine had again settled down to wait, knowing she was foolish to expect anything too soon. As

Nancy announced Mr Franklyn, her heart leapt.

She tried to read his face as he entered the drawing room. 'Mr Franklyn, what has happened? Do you have news?'

He nodded gravely. 'Maybe so. And it gives me more reason to be hopeful than the last, or I would not have troubled you again so soon. But then, I do not wish to raise false hope. Again, this could be a further instance of someone presenting what he knows we wish to hear.'

'Tell me. Please.'

'At once.' She realised he was holding a piece of folded fabric, which he now opened out a little, presenting a corner to her. 'Do you recognise this?'

The wave of joy and relief was so strong that she almost fainted.

'Yes, I do. I embroidered the letter 'C' myself.'

Those tiny stitches she had wept and hoped over — for even then, Oliver had been behaving strangely. She had hoped that with the birth of the baby he might be restored to his old self. The sight of the shawl brought back memories and feelings that were hard to bear.

William remarked in admiration, 'The stitching is so fine.'

She took a strengthening breath. 'How did you come by it?'

'That informant I was speaking to as you left.'

'Where is he?' She glanced wildly around the room, as if the man in the black hat would appear from behind the curtains. 'Is he to bring my child?'

'Not yet. This man is made of sterner stuff — which also makes me believe he may be telling the truth. But he asks for payment in advance.'

'Anything. Whatever he asks.'

William smiled. 'Come; we must make a pretence at negotiation at least.'

'But he may change his mind.'

'I doubt it. No one else will be interested in this shawl. But now you have confirmed that this does indeed belong to your child, I may proceed.'

'Wait!' she cried as he was turning to go. 'I will come with you.'

'No, Mrs Corning — I'm sorry.

'I am no longer ill. Surely I have proved that? I will do anything to retrieve my beloved son.'

'And they know this, and they will seek to use it to their advantage. Besides, he is to take me to the child. It is not a suitable location for a lady.'

She could see the sense of it, although she hated it. 'Take Ellen, at least. She has only gone quickly to her sister's house. She will be back directly.'

He said gently, 'Not even suitable for Ellen. She is a respectable girl.'

And this place was where her child might be? Madeleine bit her lip. 'If that is so, and my child is suffering such a place . . . I owe it to him — '

'Better if I go alone. Rest assured, I will have this business concluded as soon as possible and, God willing, your child once more in your arms.' His strength and steadiness were as always, reassuring.

Oh, if only that could be so. Madeleine nodded. ‘Thank you.’ She whispered after him, ‘But please, please hurry.’

6

Moving over to the window, Madeleine thought perhaps she might catch a glimpse of the constant observer as he and William met. But William was hurrying along the street and was already past the corner. Now there was only Cornelius approaching — turning his head to stare after William with a puzzled frown.

Fortunate that she had thought to look out. That gave her a few moments to collect her wits and prepare a response before Cornelius arrived.

She met his entrance with a calm smile, although her heart was thudding.

'Good morning, Cornelius.'

Should she tell him the truth? Here was the opportunity, if so.

'Who was that?' Cornelius demanded tersely of her, without ceremony.

She frowned, feigning surprise. 'Oh,

you must mean Mr Franklyn. He is merely an acquaintance of Oliver's who had only lately heard the news. He came to make his condolences.'

'No one I've ever met.'

'Nor I. But I would not expect to know all of my husband's contacts. It would not be possible.'

'I thought I knew all of them. I handled Cousin Oliver's affairs in entirety towards the end. In what respect did he claim to know him?'

'Dear me, Cornelius! What do you mean by that? It is as if you did not believe him.'

'I do not know what to believe,' Cornelius muttered. 'But you should take care. There are unscrupulous people ready to prey on wealthy widows.'

'Nothing of the sort. He came to make a brief visit, and then left. And that is an end to it.' She was becoming uneasy. Maybe this had not been a fortunate choice of deceit? Supposing as the negotiations and arrangements proceeded, Cornelius encountered Mr Franklyn again?

But no, this was foolish. All was almost done. Soon little George would be returned to her arms as William had said, and then she would tell Cornelius the truth. He would be so pleased and happy for her that he would not mind the small deception. Which had been quite justifiable because, had she told him in full, Cornelius might have felt he must hurry off to help, just when things were at a delicate stage. Better this way.

'You must be careful,' Cornelius was saying again. 'You are a tempting prospect for adventurers who might seek to wheedle their way into your affections.' He stepped closer to her, saying softly, 'Never forget that your heart is already given to me.'

She looked up at him. It would be so simple and easy to agree. But she was no longer sure whether that were true.

She said carefully, 'I do not forget. But there has been so much . . . As I told you yesterday, so much has happened.'

'I know.' His handsome face was filled with sympathy. 'There has been a lot for you to bear in a short time. But now, all that can be put behind us. All the sad memories must be swept away.' He pulled her into his arms.

She thought, *Now is the time to tell him, that my baby is one memory that does not need to be swept away. That we will soon be reunited — and can be a family together*. But yesterday she had not been at all certain that this was what Cornelius wanted.

And yet he did love her. She could not doubt that.

Once again, he was kissing her. Perhaps she should give him another chance. She tried to melt into the feelings he had always awoken in her. But no; her mind was so filled with swirling thoughts that she could not. She thought, *At this very moment, William Franklyn may be on the brink of finding my baby. I cannot think about anything else until they are both safely returned*. She broke away from his embrace.

'What is the matter?' he asked.

'We must be careful. You said so yourself. And I still feel so — unsettled.'

He smiled, and she almost regretted her lack of response. He said softly, 'Looking at you, I find it so easy to forget the proprieties. Can you blame me? I have waited for you for so long, agonising as you were given to another and so thoughtlessly. It was cruel. It almost broke my heart.'

'And mine. I know. I would have understood if you had gone far away from your cousin after that — and from me.'

'I had to keep my guard for you, watch over you. Knowing my cousin as I did. And fortunate that I was there for you when Oliver became so changed.'

'I will always be grateful for your care,' Madeleine said warmly. Who knew what might have happened if Cornelius had not been here? Her heart was filled with gratitude. How could she contemplate any other future but one spent with Cornelius? He was so good to her, so thoughtful.

He continued, 'And it is because I care for you that I seek to warn you against those who may not be so benevolent.'

Why did that faint spark of rebellion kindle within her once more? An unbidden vision of William Franklyn's smile made her heart beat more quickly. No wonder Cornelius thought her judgment could not be trusted if she was to be so easily swayed. She said meekly, 'I shall remember your warning. There is no need to worry about me.'

'If there are any other visitors you do not know — or if that visitor should return — you will be on your guard? Better by far to turn any such away than risk speaking to them.'

'Cornelius, I was only being courteous.' Her voice was almost sharp, which she regretted almost at once. She said more gently, 'I do know how to conduct myself.'

He laughed. 'But my sweet, you hardly conducted yourself with absolute propriety when you first met me.'

'I was very young. I trusted your judgment.'

'And still must. For you are promised to me. Do not forget that.' His tone was almost menacing.

Madeleine shuddered. 'Why, Cornelius, you frighten me when you glower at me like that.' She tried to keep her tone light. 'And I do not believe I made any such promise.'

'Your embraces were as good as any promise. Surely you realised that?'

'I hoped you had honourable intentions, yes. And when you spoke to my mother and was turned away, I was devastated. But I did not make any further promise. Not after that.'

'I mistook you, then.'

'No — yes. I do not know. You are confusing me.' How weak she sounded. 'Please, Cornelius, leave me alone for a while to collect myself.'

His face darkened. 'That I may not observe your supposed visits of condolence. No doubt.'

Her face was hot. He was so near the truth — and yet she could not admit that without risking spoiling it all. 'You must trust me to know what is best. That is all I can say.'

'I will leave you, in that case.'

Why was he so changeable? But soon he would understand, and all would be well. She thought, *William would have understood*. And now she was guilty of exactly what Cornelius had accused her of.

She went over to the window again as he strode away, to watch his departure, almost regretting her actions. If Cornelius turned, she would wave and summon him back. But he did not. He was striding past the familiar figure of the observer in black.

Madeleine gasped. What was that man doing there? Surely he should be escorting William to collect her child?

What had gone wrong? Now there was no doubt that he was watching the house; he was looking straight at her. She stepped back as he touched his hat, mockingly.

He was playing with them all. He knew full well whose child he held, and was hoping to gain by that.

She bit her lip, knowing suddenly and instinctively that the man wanted to do business only with her. Well, if that were so, he must have his wish. There was no alternative. Quickly, she went upstairs. She would make herself ready. She would wear the clothes she had borrowed from Ellen's sister; how fortunate that had been. This way she would not draw attention to herself. And Ellen? There was no telling how long she would be.

Madeleine paused, but only for a second or two. She would not wait. There was every chance that Ellen might object, or insist on sending for William. Both sensible attitudes, but both would waste so much time!

She took up the shawl she had embroidered and unlocked the small bureau for the second time that day. Yes, she knew the danger — but obviously something was amiss. The man's very presence here showed that.

No. Her child needed her. She could wait no longer.

She slipped out of the house without any of the servants noticing, although there was a moment in the hallway when she had to step back to avoid Nancy. At last she was outside, with the door closed softly behind her.

But her relief was short-lived. The man was nowhere in sight. She had been too long. She should not have wasted time changing her dress — although she had taken only minutes. She hurried along the paving to where the man had been standing. Was it here? By the railings? She looked up and down, gulping back a sob of frustration.

'Looking for something, lady?'

The voice was deferential but with a note of mockery. Not a voice to trust.

And how had he come up behind her so silently? But she had no choice.

'I am. Certainly. For you.'

'Dressed like a serving maid — and yet you don't speak like one. Why is that, I wonder?'

'You should have an opinion on that,' Madeleine said coldly. 'You have been watching my movements for long enough.'

'True. But there hasn't been much to watch of late. Not until the last day or two. I was thinking I was wasting my time.'

'Please. What do you want?'

'So you noticed me at last and sent your cove to sort me out. But not good enough, see? I told him, 'I want to deal with the mother,' I said. 'She'll know best what is due to her poor little baby'.'

'So you do have him?'

'I didn't say that.'

'But you know where he is? You sent his shawl — this shawl. I recognised the embroidery.'

'I have no doubt of it. And if we can come to some mutual agreement as to payment, then I'm sure something can be done.'

'You will have suitable payment. As I am sure Mr Franklyn has told you.'

'Oh, yes. But his idea of payment, when he has nothing to do with the child — and yours, as the mother — may differ. If you take my meaning.' He set off down the street at an almost leisurely pace and she followed blindly, hardly noticing where he was leading her.

She answered cautiously, 'That may well be.' Her heart beating faster as beneath her cloak, her hand tightened against the coins in her pocket.

'I'm right in supposing, then, that he does have nothing to do with it? This Mr Franklyn.'

She frowned. 'I do not understand you.' And then, as he tilted his head with a knowing wink, she did understand and her face was hot. 'Of course he does not. I am a widow now, but I was married when our child was born.'

'That don't always follow. And I ask myself, how has this come about? Why should your husband be in such a hurry to dispose of the child?'

She said sharply, 'I was not then acquainted with Mr Franklyn. He is working for me, to return my child. It is strictly a business arrangement.'

'And yet you doesn't feel you can trust him to get on with it on his own? I thought as much. It's a wicked, cruel world, Missus.'

'May we please keep to the matter in hand?' Belatedly she took note of her surroundings and gasped. They were away from the major road, which led to a bridge over the Thames — and how quickly things had changed.

Underfoot there was mud and filth. Thin figures, as pale as shadows, lounged at corners or huddled in doorways. She avoided looking at them directly, aware of how they were staring at her. But why was she so fearful? The poor used the ordinary thoroughfares as often as she did; she was accustomed to seeing them. Or not seeing them, because that was what you learned to do. But here there were so many all together, and the gables almost met overhead, shutting out the sun. The air smelled sour. And worst, this was their place — and she felt as if she had no business here.

A ragged child stepped into her path, eyes wide, hands outstretched, whining, 'Please, Missus.'

Madeleine shivered, all too conscious of the money she held. 'I've dressed plainly. How do they know?'

The man laughed. 'It's an instinct. Poverty will always call, one to another. They know their own.'

She said quickly, 'I'll need your escort out again. I'll not pay otherwise.'

'I think you will. I have the trump card, don't I? But don't worry, I'll fetch you out again. No good killing the goose. As you might say.'

She dared not consider the oddity of that remark at present. She just wanted this to be done with.

Running footsteps sounded behind them. Madeleine turned swiftly in alarm — and could have wept with relief. 'Ellen!'

'Whatever are you doing? No,' as Madeleine began to speak, 'I can see what. It's lucky I caught sight of you. Why didn't you wait for me?'

'I had to act quickly and I didn't know how long you would be.'

'The more the merrier,' her escort remarked, touching his hat to Ellen. 'Many hands give the lightest work. So to speak. Down here, ladies.' He turned swiftly down an alley that seemed even dingier than the street — if indeed that were possible.

'Many more twists and turns and we'll never find the way out of this place,' Ellen muttered.

'I have made arrangements,' Madeleine assured her.

The man hooted. 'That you have. But no need for alarm, because here we are.' He gestured to a dark doorway with a pretence at politeness, and laughed again as Madeleine took a step back. 'Well, maybe not. I'll go first. Mrs Ticklepenny, there. You have visitors.'

The woman he addressed was bobbing and rubbing her hands together with what must be intended as a smile fixed upon her sharp face. But her eyes were darting and shifting over them.

'Where is he?' Madeleine said. She stared around the room and recoiled in horror. What she had taken for several piles of dirty rags scattered on the bare floor were actually moving. Faint whining cries betrayed that each heap held a baby. And one cry in particular seared her heart. She turned at once to a pile that might have been slightly less dirty, and snatched him up.

'You knows him. That's the one. Don't it warm the heart?' the woman said, her voice heavy with sarcasm.

'Yes, oh, yes.' Tears came to Madeleine's eyes. This was her son!

Ellen murmured urgently, 'What about the mark?'

Madeleine shook her head, trying to say that there was no need. Unable to speak through her feelings of joy and relief.

'I think we should,' Ellen insisted.

Yes, of course they should. What would William Franklyn say if they had not? She smiled shakily as she began to uncover the infant's feet. Her son protested as the cold air hit his limbs, not at all grateful for her discovery. As if in sympathy, the other babies wailed also.

'Satisfied?' Their escort was grinning. 'I'm due payment, it seems. As agreed.' He turned to Mrs Ticklepenny irritably. 'Can't you quiet that rabble? Can't hear myself think.'

The woman raised her fist to the nearest child, growling a threat.

'No!' Madeleine cried. 'Don't you dare touch them.'

The woman shrugged and glared. 'Why should you care? These are nothing to do with you.'

'I know — but whose are they? Not

all yours, surely?' They seemed of too similar an age, as far as she could tell.

'They're mine now I'm paid to care for them. Just as I was with yours. And well cared for he's been, as you see. Not a mark or a bruise on him.'

Madeleine shuddered, doubting whether the same could be said of the other poor mites. 'You are paid regularly? The parents watch over them?'

The woman shrieked with laughter. 'No. Paid once. So they'd be out of sight and out of mind. Inconveniences as often as not. Know what I mean? No one cares whether they live or die.'

'Come now,' the man said. 'Enough talk. Let's see your money.'

Madeleine passed him what she had brought and reached out her arms.

The woman laughed. 'Not so fast. Safe passage is extra.'

Madeleine stared at her. She realised suddenly how vulnerable they were — and they had to get back safely with baby George.

'You must return with us and I shall

pay you then,' she offered.

The man said, 'There's no problem with that. I know where you live. I'm practised in waiting. I can wait outside as long as you like.'

Madeleine nodded. Everything would work out. It must. She had had little need of money to date, beyond an awareness that shopkeepers and tradesmen would send their bills — to Oliver, of course. Or Cornelius. But she had her jewellery. Surely he would be satisfied with some of that? Just let them get safely back. That was what mattered.

7

They made their way through the narrow alleys; Madeleine with little George, Ellen close beside her and then the foster mother, if she could be called that, who had insisted on coming too. The man acted as escort as before, but now carried a stout stick in one hand.

They caused a stir amongst the huddled poor as they passed. One or two called out in greeting but were swiftly silenced by a look or a wave of the stick. Again, Madeleine could only feel grateful to him. But all this was as if happening in some other world. She was all too joyfully aware of the small weight in her arms, the blue eyes at first blinking warily, only to close in contented sleep with the soothing rhythm of their walking motion.

As they came to the familiar square, however, the affability vanished. The man put out a hand. 'You go in alone. He stays here, with your girl.'

Madeleine's eyes widened in shock. 'Why? I have said I will pay.' She could not bear to give him up again, even for a few minutes. Her arms tightened and the baby, waking, whimpered.

'I am sure you will. But this way, there's no doubt and we're all happy.'

'I'll take care of him,' Ellen said tersely. 'You go in.'

Unwillingly Madeleine passed her baby to Ellen and climbed the steps, hardly thinking straight. Only knowing that she must hurry, hurry and hold him in her arms again.

Time seemed to stand still. She felt as if her limbs were leaden, just when she needed to move swiftly. Oliver's desk, once more, where she found some coins she had missed. Upstairs to her jewellery box. What to take? Corning family pieces that must be kept in trust for George's wife, surely. Gifts from her parents — oh, she could not part with those — the rift with her mother still hurt so deeply. But there were all these pieces Oliver had given to her in the first happy days of their marriage and engagement. Surely they would suffice? She snatched them up.

And thank goodness, the three figures were still waiting on the pavement — Ellen staunchly jigging her precious charge; the thin-faced woman saying impatiently, 'I tell you, that's the last we'll see of her.'

'Aha!' The man turned as the door opened. 'What have you brought?'

She pressed the coins and jewellery into his hands and turned to take baby George.

'Just a minute.' His eyes were alight with greed. 'Not bad — for an ordinary transaction. But not where a precious son and heir is concerned. I can see how you feel about him. He's worth more than these baubles, surely, wouldn't you say?'

She knew her mistake at once. She should have followed Franklyn's sound advice. Now she had lost any advantage she might have had. She did not know what to do. Of course she would pay anything — anything — to have her child restored to her. And she had foolishly betrayed her feelings all too easily. If only William Franklyn were here. She tried to speak sharply.

'This is all I am paying. This is far more than we agreed.'

'But we didn't agree, did we? Not proper, like. And we can just as easy take him back.' He made as if to snatch the child.

Madeleine held on tightly. 'No, no! Please.'

Ellen tried to come between them. 'Don't listen to him. Who else would pay him anything at all? Your baby is only precious to you.'

The man snarled, 'Who knows what I might do if crossed?'

'You don't want to cross him, Missus,' the woman cried.

A deep, angry voice cut across them. 'What is going on?'

Madeleine turned thankfully. Had

her thoughts brought William in some miraculous way? But she was almost equally relieved to see Cornelius.

'Cornelius! How glad I am that you are here. I had an arrangement with this person — and now he is asking more than we ever agreed.'

The man's eyes moved from Cornelius' face to hers and back again. 'Nothing to worry about. Just a misunderstanding,' he muttered.

'I cannot see how you could possibly have any kind of agreement with this lady,' Cornelius growled.

Madeleine said quickly, 'But I did. That is not in question. It is merely the exact nature of the payment . . . ' Madeleine bit her lip. The decision not to confide fully in Cornelius was now shown to be folly.

He said, ignoring her, 'You will take no payment from this lady for whatever reason.'

She realised that the man had already pocketed the jewellery and that the woman was nowhere in sight. 'Forget I spoke, Missus. Everything's quite all right as it is.'

Cornelius seized his arm. 'Wait! I demand to know what this is about.'

Madeleine tried to pull him away. 'No, you do not understand. Truly, it does not matter.' *Please*, she thought, *just let the man go*. She never wanted to see him again.

Cornelius dropped his hold and the man melted away into the passers-by as if he had never been there. Cornelius frowned after him for a moment and then turned his attention to Madeleine. 'So now will you answer my question?' His voice was almost menacing.

The baby, half hidden beneath Madeleine's plain shawl, gave a whimper and Cornelius' head swivelled towards the sound.

'Ah — I see.' There was fury in his voice.

She thought, *He is angry because I put myself in danger*. She said, 'Yes, I have my son back. Is not that wonderful? See.' She uncovered the small face. 'There.' She gave a shaky laugh. 'I am afraid that he needs a wash.'

A range of expressions crossed Cornelius' face. 'But — this is preposterous. You cannot possibly be certain that this urchin is yours. How can you? I know of that man. I know him for a villain and a rogue.'

'Oh, but I am. Beyond all doubt. I knew at once. And there is the birthmark on his foot.'

'I cannot believe this.' His face was dark with anger.

Madeleine faced him squarely, although inside she was shaking. This was not the Cornelius she knew. Why did he not understand?

She said quietly, 'It is not appropriate to conduct this discussion in the street, cousin. Let us go inside.'

Cornelius exhaled deeply and nodded. He offered her his arm. 'Give — *that* — to the maid.'

It was that dismissive tone that convinced her. She could never love

Cornelius. Perhaps she never had.

'No, thank you,' she replied gravely. 'I will never let him go.'

It was with reluctance that she thought better of that maternal impulse and knew that she must hand her son over to Nancy when they reached the hall. She wanted only to be rid of Cornelius and tend to her child herself. But that would be ungrateful. Cornelius would have to be told the full story. And surely he would understand how much this meant to her?

She said to Nancy, 'Ellen will explain. I will come up when I can.' Tenderly she kissed the small face.

'How can you do such a thing?' Cornelius spat, with a look of disgust. 'The brat is utterly filthy.'

'Through no fault of his own,' Madeleine answered quietly. 'Pray come into the drawing room.'

The door was hardly closed behind them before Cornelius began.

'I have been away too long. That is

very clear. And I went only wanting to ensure your affairs were in order, as always. And this is what happens. I find you having speech with the ragtag and worst sorts from the lowest lanes of the city.' He clenched a fist.

'Please allow me to speak, Cornelius. I am grateful for the work you have done, yes, but do not pretend any noble motive. You believed that you were working for our future together and therefore for yourself.'

'Of course. You have always known that.'

'But I am beginning to feel that you saw my child — Oliver's child — as having no part in that future.'

'That child is gone. You must accept that. And it is only right and fitting that it be so. Oliver Corning was to have no long-term part in our lives. That was what we agreed.'

'I do not recall making such an agreement; if I did, it was not an honourable one and I take no pride in it. I am older now and can see that more clearly. Having bowed, reluctantly, to my mother's strictures, I took the inevitable course and did my best to be a dutiful and loving wife. And I came to love Oliver in a way. A different love to the way I felt about you.'

She shook her head. Even relating this was still painful for her. 'I do not know what turned him against me, so unaccountably.'

'How should that matter when your marriage turned out to be so brief?'

She ignored his comment. 'But my love for my child is different again, and cannot ever be denied or given up.'

'Nonsense. Most women accept the inevitability of infant mortality. Why should you be different? These are the ramblings of a weak and female mind. This is why you women need men to care for you.'

Madeleine breathed deeply, trying to contain her anger. 'You have only hardened the decision I had already made — but not admitted to myself. Cornelius, you can have no further part in my life. And I am sorry, but this is the last time you will enter my house.'

His face was dark, his eyes almost wild. He took a step towards her, half raising his arm. She thought that he might be about to strike her but she stood firm, without flinching.

There was a tap at the door. 'Mr William Franklyn to see you, Madam,' the butler announced. 'Shall I ask him to wait?'

'No,' Madeleine answered. 'Please show him in.'

Surely, she thought, William must sense the tension in the room? He gave no sign of it as the men acknowledged each other with slight bows, William with a pleasant smile, Cornelius frowning. Madeleine made the introductions but Cornelius hardly allowed her to finish.

'I almost encountered you the other day, Franklyn. Are you come to renew your condolences? A widow must always prove an attraction.'

'You overreach yourself,' Madeleine

said, with icy calm.

William said, 'I merely wondered if I might be of any assistance.'

'Not unless you have nursing skills, it would seem,' Cornelius said bitterly. 'But I see it now. This is all your doing.'

'Cornelius, you will please leave. As you were about to do.'

Madeleine rang the bell.

'Very well.' Cornelius spoke in a tight and furious voice. 'Do not doubt but that you have made an enemy, Franklyn.'

William's tone was mild. 'That was not my intention. I have no ill-will toward you. Why should I? I regret that you seem to have mistaken me. Come, let us part as friends.' William held out his hand.

Cornelius turned away and flung the door open upon a surprised maidservant. He pushed past her, snatched up his hat and slammed the outer door behind him.

'I am so sorry that you had to experience that,' Madeleine murmured.

'There is no need for you to apologise.' He stepped quickly towards her. 'Why, your hands are shaking.' And suddenly, before either of them had realised what was happening, his arms were round her and she was relaxing blissfully into the warmth of his hold. He said softly, 'I gather there was some commitment between you? You are too good for him.'

'It is not his fault, in a way. I was so young. He was led to expect — ' She sighed. 'But so much has happened since then. I was mistaken in him.'

'Hush.' He almost whispered the word, so that it seemed an endearment. 'You do not have to explain.'

And then he was kissing her — and her lips responded deliriously to his.

They drew apart at last, and Madeleine was staring at him in surprised realisation. This was so different to anything she had known.

William said, 'I should apologise, but I cannot. I am not sorry.' He smiled.

She answered breathlessly, 'Oh, do

not. Because neither am I.' She knew now that she had known from the first moment of seeing him — that this would be no chance encounter, as quickly forgotten. She had recognised something in him that resounded in the depths of her heart.

'And now I have something to tell you.'

'And I have so much to tell you.'

'I thought you might. Did I hear a child's cry as I came through the hall? From the upper rooms?'

'Oh, yes.' She thought the joy would burst from her. 'Oh, Mr Franklyn — I have my son. But please, you are not to be angry with me. I know I was to wait — but I could not. I was so afraid your informant would disappear and never come back. That I would lose my only chance. And when he said — '

'I am not angry. I knew I should never have placed you in that position. But if anything had happened to you, I would so deeply have blamed myself. But I was delayed by — ' He paused.

'By my own family concerns, yet again, which I may not speak of as yet. It is not my secret to tell.'

'Would you like to see him?'

'Of course. My love, I am hoping that our paths may move onward together. He is part of your life, and therefore of mine.'

Madeleine rang the bell. Could William love another man's son? She recalled Cornelius Corning's grim rejection and shuddered. In a way she could comprehend it, she supposed; of course a man would wish his own bloodline to succeed him — but Cornelius had been unnecessarily cruel.

'Ellen, could we see my son? Is he bathed and dressed yet?' A pleasure she would have gladly shared herself if Cornelius had not arrived. But now she could look forward to performing such tasks many times.

Ellen smiled. 'He is sound asleep now. He was exhausted. But I can bring him down if you wish.'

'No, no,' William Franklyn said quickly. 'We must not disturb him. 'Perhaps we might go up and see him?'

Little George was sleeping peacefully in the cradle that had so recently been left empty. William stepped over to look down at him. 'I would have known him without the cradle — and the birthmark he must have. He is like you. It is the shape of the nose, I believe.'

'Do you not think all babies look much the same?'

'Not this one,' he said softly, so only she could hear it. 'Not the one that belongs to the woman I love.'

She looked down at the baby, longing to seize him in her arms — but no, she must contain herself when he was sleeping. He had had little enough opportunity for comfortable rest of late.

'Come,' she said regretfully. 'We must not disturb him.'

They left the room and went downstairs. Madeleine said sadly, 'But it was a dreadful place. And there were other children there. At least three or four. I hated having to leave them there, to suffer.'

William said gravely, 'I guessed as much. So, before you ask — yes, I am sure I can make better arrangements for them. Leave the matter with me.'

She stared at him in admiration. 'Is there anything you cannot arrange?'

William laughed. 'In your case, I was not allowed to do very much. No matter.' He paused. 'I wonder — the poor child looks so peaked and pinched. Do you think he might benefit from some fresh country air?'

'Oh, indeed yes. That is just what I would like. But when Oliver was ill, he had allowed the Yorkshire estate to become very run-down. Even before that, he showed little interest in going there after our marriage. Cornelius had been to see it, to make a report. Unfortunately I did not have time to examine his findings. But I suspect that it might not be suitable for a baby straight away. And,' she added sadly, 'I cannot go home, of course.

That house was ideal for children but there has been no word from my mother since — she chose to believe Oliver's allegations.'

'I believe I may have a solution to your problem.'

'You do?' She gazed at him in amazement.

'Indeed, yes. I know of a good woman with two children of her own who has fallen upon difficult times. She lives in a small house in a rural setting but with sufficient rooms. And it is no great distance from your own estate, which could prove convenient.'

'Oh, it sounds ideal! And if suitable — for I would wish to see it myself — I would pay her well, of course.' She thought, *Perhaps we can all go. Somewhere new, away from this house and all the unpleasant memories. And away from Cornelius, too*. She shivered. Yes, he had left and had seemed to accept his dismissal. But would he find it so easy to let go of everything he had planned?

Suddenly she wanted to be gone. At once. She trusted William instinctively. If he recommended this woman, she was sure that everything would be all right.

8

The decision took no more than a moment. Madeleine declared, 'London will soon be unbearably hot and unhealthy; at its worst for a small child. I believe we should go — just as soon as it may be arranged. 'She felt that her voice sounded high and brittle; no doubt her fears were foolish. But Cornelius' veiled threat was hanging heavily in her mind.

William gave her a questioning look but said only, 'I will escort you, if I may? I am completely at your disposal.'

It was the first time she had ever attempted such a task, needing so much organisation. Yet everything moved so easily that she could hardly believe it. Dazzling prospects opened before her. She could sell Oliver's London house with its dark memories, and start afresh. After they were married she and

William could be together with little George in a new home.

She thought, *He has not yet asked me*. But she was certain that he would. No honourable man would take her in his arms as William had without being ready to propose marriage. Unbidden, the idea came that Cornelius had also held her in his arms. *Forget Cornelius!* she scolded herself. She never wanted to see him again. And he was a capable and ingenious worker with many contacts. He would soon find something else to do. Maybe a suitable heiress. She tried to produce a smile at the thought but could not.

'Are you all right?' William's voice was soft with concern.

'Yes, of course. But I would very much like to leave as soon as we may.'

As the hours and days passed with no sign of Cornelius making any attempt to carry out his threats, she was able to forget about him. At last they were ready, having managed to confine herself and her son, with accompanying servants and baggage, to only three vehicles. William had proved himself to be a master of organisation in dealing with the hire of horses and conveyances.

And the day was here. She entered the carriage she was sharing with Ellen and baby George with a sigh of relief. William had last-minute business of his own to attend to and was to join them on horseback as they moved out of London. She smiled at the thought of seeing him again, her heart beating faster — although she had seen him only the day before.

She leaned towards the window for a last view of the house, taking pleasure in her intention never to live there again. This was truly a new beginning for them all.

On the corner stood a dark-coated figure, making no attempt to disguise his presence — staring after the little procession with a threatening frown. Cornelius! She sank back onto the cushions with a hand to her throat, and now her heart was pounding unpleasantly. There was no mistake. He had wanted to ensure that she saw him.

She had been wrong. He had not forgotten.

* * *

She had sent a message ahead to the house at Brierley so that the housekeeper would be prepared for their arrival. They could stay there temporarily, which would give her the opportunity to meet the lady William had recommended — and for her to have time to prepare for them in her turn. If she should be agreeable to the arrangement, of course.

They were all weary after the long journey. Madeleine wanted nothing more than to see her child safely installed, to have a light meal herself and a long rest. But as they entered the hallway, she smelled an earthy odour that made her think of rotting leaves.

'Damp,' William stated.

She stopped, horrified. 'I had no idea. And Cornelius was here less than a month ago. Whatever has happened here?' She turned to the housekeeper.

'I've had to manage on my own.' The woman seemed wary. 'With little Jenny; she being pikestaff plain.'

Madeleine shook her head. 'I don't understand. Did Mr Cornelius not make suitable arrangements? Where are the rest of the staff?'

'They wouldn't stay. Not with the goings-on here. Not when their wages weren't forthcoming. He gathered a crowd of wastrels around him, drinking and gaming every night.' She added defensively, 'And that accounts for the broken windows in the drawing room.'

'We cannot stay, either,' Madeleine decided. 'This is not a suitable place for a baby. Where is the nearest inn?'

'We can go on to Eastfield House,' William suggested. 'I will instruct your coachmen of the direction and ride ahead.'

It hardly seemed fair. But there was

little alternative. Ellen was already, without complaint, retracing her steps.

Madeleine addressed the housekeeper. 'I will return shortly. Tomorrow, hopefully — and certainly the next day. I must sort everything out. This house must be made habitable again.' She could not understand why Cornelius had done nothing — had made things worse, if the housekeeper was to be believed. She had been sadly mistaken in him; more than she had realised. Misled by good looks and stolen embraces, when he could not be relied on.

'Mrs Gibbons — on no account is Mr Cornelius to return here,' she declared. 'I have already dismissed him.' And, she thought, one of her first tasks would be to hire some strong grooms and footmen to make sure that her wishes could be enforced.

'I am not going far,' she told the old woman. 'Only to — ' What was the name? Ah, yes. 'Eastfield House. Just outside the village of Eastgate.'

'Indeed, yes. Poor lady.' The housekeeper nodded. 'You mean Mrs Franklyn as should be? Or, as some say, may be already.'

'No — I do not think . . . ' Madeleine stared at her. The housekeeper had seemed lucid enough. But here was Ellen to say that all was bestowed again and ready to leave. And what was to be gained by questioning the woman further? Madeleine's mind was swimming. She needed to think. She must ask William as soon as he rejoined them.

She said little to Ellen as they set off once again. Looking at her sympathetically, Ellen ventured, 'A wearisome nuisance, but it can't be far.'

Madeleine merely nodded, her mind taken up with what she would say.

And too soon, it seemed, the coach slowed and William was tapping on the window. 'It is all arranged. She does not mind. I knew she would not.'

'William — you said her name was Spenceley. But the housekeeper called her Mrs Franklyn.'

To her surprise, he laughed. 'So you have heard already? I should have known. Secrets cannot be kept in the country, whatever my father might believe. But we will speak of it no more at present if you do not mind, for I have sworn secrecy and must keep my word.'

Madeleine shook her head. She did mind — but could not ask. Who was this lady? Surely — her heart was beating painfully — she could not be William's secret wife? Not when he had declared his love for her? And if that were the case, he would never take her to meet the lady! Would he? She yawned. She was so tired; she was hardly thinking straight.

She put a hand over her eyes. But what if her judgment should be sadly at fault? Once, she had been very certain of Cornelius — and only see how mistaken she had been. And what about baby George? She must always consider his welfare and security, whatever she did.

And here they were — arrived at a neat grey house surrounded by lilac and honeysuckle, As the vehicles drew up, the door opened and with a flurry of wide arms and auburn hair, their hostess ran to greet them. 'Come in, come in. We are all ready for you. You must be wearied to death, on those bumps and ruts all day. And this must be your little one. Bless you, my sweet. Oh, so thin. Never mind, we will soon alter that.' Her laughter was warm and joyous and in spite of her fears, Madeleine could not help smiling.

'And Sarah,' William was saying when he could make himself heard. 'This is Madeleine, who will be staying here with you until she decides what to do over at Brierley.'

Madeleine gasped as both she and George were clasped in Sarah's arms. 'I have heard so much about you — and your sad story. And your baby is adorable. But what am I thinking of? Come in and sit down — we have had rooms made ready as soon as we had word you were coming. And refreshments before you sleep?'

An army could descend and Sarah Spenceley would think nothing of it. One could not help liking her, if not loving her. And how could William not help it, either? And his easy use of Sarah's first name had pierced her heart. But Madeleine knew she must be practical. Here was a warm and loving refuge and she could only welcome that.

Now she was occupied with the bustle of getting the baby, servants and baggage inside and seeing the rooms they were to occupy. At one point, she came out onto the landing in search of Ellen, and paused. William and Sarah were standing closely together, lit by the lamp at the top of the stairs. Sarah was looking up earnestly into his face, saying softly, 'Do you think we may achieve it, at last?'

He said, 'I have every hope of it. I only need to convince my father.'

Sarah took a breath that was almost a

sob. 'It has been so long.'

Madeleine slid back, unseen, into the room. She was shaking. What could this mean?

Within a very short time, it seemed, little George was sleeping peacefully in a comfortable cradle and Madeleine had leisure to consider her own situation. 'I am so looking forward to our getting to know each other,' Sarah told her. 'I am sure we will be good friends.'

Madeleine tried to smile. 'I am afraid I cannot talk now. I must sleep.'

'Of course. What am I thinking of? You are only just recovered from your illness. William told me a little of your story, I hope you don't mind.'

'Not at all,' Madeleine said politely, gazing about her. 'Where is William?'

'I am here.' William spoke cheerfully enough as he came into the room but he was holding a folded paper in one hand. 'I am sorry — I have to see my father. I had hoped to spend my time here in helping you — but with my father, everything is always of the first urgency.'

Sarah laughed wryly. 'Oh, that is too bad. He is always aware of everything that happens in the family. I don't know how he manages it.'

'You must go, of course,' Madeleine said quickly. After all, William had so generously given his attention to her concerns that he had had little time for his own. In fact, she knew very little about him or what his circumstances might be. She shook her head. Would she never learn? Bestowing her heart on such a brief acquaintance — yet again.

'All the same,' William said firmly, 'he must wait. I will set the most urgent matters in train for you. I have local knowledge and can engage men for you who will be trustworthy. Your safety is the most important thing.'

'My safety? Oh, I see. But surely you do not think that Cornelius will follow us here?'

'Probably not. I am merely taking

care to protect you; all of you.' His smile included Sarah who smiled back and murmured that she must see to the children. William said, 'There is nothing for Cornelius here. I am sure he must recognise that now and accept it.'

Madeleine strove to be practical. 'You will not be gone for long. I presume your father lives nearby?'

'I am afraid not. But it is less than half a day's ride.'

She frowned, wishing she could rid herself of the immense weariness sweeping over her. 'But surely — is Eastfield House not part of your estate?'

'Ah — I see how you might think so. But it is mine, through a legacy from my mother.'

'But . . . ' There was so much she did not understand.

'Hush. If I say more, I will be encroaching upon what I must not speak of. Not yet. You must be patient, my love. Trust me.'

And when he kissed her, she knew

that she did trust him. With William before her, so strong and steadfast, she could easily believe in him.

* * *

In spite of her weariness, Madeleine did not sleep well. She could not banish that picture of William and Sarah standing together, Sarah's hand on his arm, so intimately.

In the early hours of the morning, she came to a decision. She must begin work on the house at once, so that they might all move in as soon as possible. Whatever had happened in the past between William and Sarah, it was best that she should not stay here, under Sarah's roof. She tossed and turned for hours before falling into a deep sleep with the dawn.

Sarah seemed surprised by her purpose. 'But so soon? You are welcome to stay here as long as you like. At least wait until William returns.'

'Returns? He has left already?'

'He has found the men for you, as promised. He was up at first light, setting everything in train. But you were sleeping so deeply, Ellen told us, and looked so flushed that she did not like to wake you.'

Madeleine fought the tears. Why had he not waited? She was so much better now. There had been no need to let her sleep through his departure.

'We were thinking of what would be best for you,' Sarah said gently.

'Yes. I do see that. The sooner to leave, the sooner he will be back. But I am determined that I shall press on with the repairs in William's absence. It is time I acted on my own account instead of relying on others to be strong for me. I am taking too great an advantage of the good nature of others.'

'I don't think William sees that as a chore.'

Madeleine hesitated. Was she merely acting upon the irrational fantasies of the night? An overtired mind whirling incessantly and drawing the wrong conclusions? A brief knock before two small boys ran into the room, their faces gleeful. 'Mamma, can we play with the baby?'

Sarah laughed and scooped them up into her arms. 'Of course. He will want to play with you too, soon. He is very little, though.'

Madeleine hardly heard what Sarah was saying. She was staring at the older child's face. His resemblance to William was unmistakable.

She said, 'No, thank you. You are very kind, but I have so much to do. I must speak to these men of William's and seek out and re-engage the staff who left. I must reassure them that there will be no repetition of whatever has been going on.' She was hardly aware of what she was saying or whether it made sense. 'I would like to sell Brierley eventually. But it is my son's inheritance, after all.'

'I understand,' Sarah answered softly. 'Inheritance is a difficult matter.'

Madeleine was convinced that she was right. William and Sarah were bound together, whether married or not, through these beautiful children — and William's father was reluctant to accept the union. She understood it all clearly now. No wonder William had gone to see the old man and Sarah was so concerned.

She said, her voice shaking, 'You seem to speak from the heart?'

Sarah shook her head. 'Oh, my dear, I would so wish to confide in you. But I have sworn to speak of my problems to no one. As soon as I am able, I promise you will be one of the first to know. I love you like a sister already.'

Madeleine felt as though her heart was breaking. She did not want to be Sarah's, and therefore William's, sister. But how could she have so misunderstood William's feelings towards her? Perhaps because so much had happened over the past few weeks that she could no longer view anything in a sensible and balanced way.

It was fortunate, she thought as she returned to the house, that she had this to take her attention. Hard work would at least give her no opportunity for dark thoughts.

9

Over the next few days Madeleine threw herself into arranging and even participating in the work at Brierley. This proved a welcome diversion. She was grateful for the men William had hired, and felt safe with them in and around the house. And it seemed that one evening when she was absent, safely at Eastfield with baby George, the rowdies who had broken the windows tried to return — but were soon sent packing. There was no further trouble after that.

There was no sign of Cornelius. He must have accepted things and decided to make a new life for himself. She was relieved and grateful.

But as the refurbishment work was at last almost finished, with no news of William's return, she knew she must come to a decision. The more she considered her situation, the more she came to doubt William's declaration of love and those heady few days when she had thought she could rejoice in loving him and being loved in return. This could not go on. If she sold the house, she would be able to move far away from the distress of seeing Sarah and William together.

But little George was flourishing so wonderfully here, growing plumper and happier each day. An idea came to her. She could make Brierley into a home for abandoned children from London; it would be a well-run and loving refuge for them. She could throw herself into making it so. A welcome distraction from troubles of the heart.

And in spite of all her doubts and fears, she was loving the deep contentment of rediscovering her child.

She must not stay long at the house today, she thought. Despite the way his health and weight had improved, baby George had seemed a little fretful that morning so she had left him at Sarah's house — instead of bringing Ellen to Brierley to have him with her all day. Perhaps he might be sickening for something? Although Ellen had opined that he was only teething, and Sarah's boys did not seem to be affected.

She heard the sound of wheels outside. There — she knew she should not have left him. They had sent for her. She hurried out.

Millward was opening the door; she glimpsed a small closed carriage before turning anxiously to the soberly dressed stranger on the steps.

Could it be? A long-forgotten pain clutched her heart. 'I am Mrs Corning. Do you have a message for me?'

He bowed, 'Indeed. From Rush-wood.'

How she had longed for her mother to send word — or even to respond to her letters. But she knew at once that this must be bad news.

'You had better come into the drawing room,' Almost before the door was closed, she asked quickly. 'What is it? What has happened?'

'Your mother is seriously ill — and has asked for you.'

'Ill?' she repeated. A moment of joy; this must mean that she was forgiven. Followed by the deeper sorrow that this must mean that they would not be reunited for long. If only she might be in time!

'I will come at once. Can you take me?'

'Of course. Those were my instructions.'

She was thinking swiftly as she hurried upstairs to gather her bonnet and cloak. 'If we go first to Eastfield House — I will direct you — I will pack a few things and bring a maid.' She would not submit baby George to the jolting lanes at present — nor to a household where there was illness. Ellen must stay with him to care for him — but Nancy would be as good.

She had hoped to question the messenger further, after giving the directions to Eastfield, but he swung up onto the box beside the driver at once. She did not recognise either of them, but some servants found her mother a demanding employer and no doubt there had been many changes since Madeleine had left home.

She gathered her cloak around her as they set off. How long had her mother been ill? It must indeed be serious for this man to be sent for her and for her mother to undergo this amazing change of heart. Would she still be alive when Madeleine got there? She hoped so — so much — but at least her mother had asked for her, and that was a thought to be cherished.

They were setting a good pace. She glanced out of the window at a particularly sharp turn and frowned. She had been too much taken up with her own thoughts. Surely they should have reached Eastfield by now? She banged on the roof. They jolted to a halt.

'This is not the way to Eastgate village.'

The man seemed concerned. 'I am sorry, Madam. I quite thought there had been a change of plan — that your housekeeper was to send for your maid and belongings to follow on. I understood that she had told you. Otherwise we would be travelling in the wrong direction entirely — at a time when every minute could count, if you are to see your mother alive.'

'That is what I wish, of course. We must make all possible speed. But I don't recall . . . ' She was certain that the housekeeper had said nothing of that. But her words were lost as the door was closed and the horses whipped up. It did make sense. She had to agree. This way there could be no delay. No point in wondering how the mistake had been made; she must concentrate on seeing her mother and what she would say to her, for what might be their last meeting.

She did not recognise the passing countryside, but would not expect to. She had never taken this route, between her childhood home and Oliver's house. Once they were married, they had driven straight to London. Happier times! She had been unwilling and fearful, and Oliver had been so kind . . . In spite of her worries, or maybe because of them, the jolting motion was sending her into a fitful doze.

Some time later, she came to, not knowing how long she had slept. Where were they? She peered out of the window. They must have been travelling for an hour or more, at least. Surely they must be within reach of her childhood surroundings by now?

She thought, *They have mistaken the way. We have wasted so much time* — and was raising her hand to the roof again when the coach jerked to a halt. She frowned, glimpsing trees and maybe a modest house set back from the track, in the shadows.

The door was flung open by a burly figure who, again, she did not know. 'Come, Madam. Step out.'

She did so and at once the hand

reaching out to help her alight was grasping her arm tightly. She said, 'Where is this? Has my mother been brought here? Is she infectious?'

'All will be explained once we are inside.'

'I demand that you explain now.' She tried to pull herself free. 'Where is my mother? Are my sisters with her?'

'I know nothing of any mother,' the man said shortly. 'A party to be looked after is all I know, and that's what I'll do.'

'No!' Terror swept through her. Cornelius! His hand must be in this. Why had she been so eager to dismiss and forget him?

She began to struggle, as violently as she could, and let out a scream.

'Help! Help me someone. Please.'

'What is all this?' A woman's voice now. A voice she knew.

'Oh, thank goodness. Nurse Herries! You must help me.'

'Deal with her, husband. At once.'

And Madeleine felt a sharp pain at

the back of her head, before everything was dark.

* * *

It was as if the preceding weeks had never been. She was lying on a bed with an all-too familiar face and form leaning over her. 'Ah — you are awake. And just in time to take your medicine.'

Madeleine's head was aching. She could not think properly. But here was Nurse Herries. And her baby was gone, and Oliver was dead. Everything other than that were dreams and falsehood.

No! She was certain of the truth. No one could tell her otherwise. She had escaped, found her baby, seen through Cornelius, fallen in love . . . She would not be deceived and entrapped again.

She said weakly, 'Thank you.' As she was lifted to the cup, the pain in her head jarred suddenly. Without thinking, she moved her hand and the cup spilled its contents onto the blanket.

Nurse jumped back, startled. 'You

little fiend. So that's your game? Let me tell you, you may have tricked me last time but you will not do so again.'

'I am sorry,' Madeleine gasped, trying to sound as feeble as possible. 'My hands failed me, I did not intend it.'

'No matter. There is plenty more, make no mistake. I will call Mr Herries to hold your hands if necessary. There will be no more unfortunate accidents. Mr Herries and I are very experienced in caring for invalids.'

'Indeed you are.' Not the unpleasant Mr Herries, but a voice Madeleine knew all too well. And now her hands did indeed jerk in shock as she clutched them to her face. Cornelius came into the room.

'I must thank you for all your endeavours, Nurse. You have done very well indeed. But I believe that our invalid will not be requiring her medicinal draught today.'

'Are you sure of that, sir? I believe she may be troublesome without it.'

'Maybe later.' He smiled grimly. 'But for now I need her to attend to what I am about to say.'

'Just a little? So that she may attend to you quietly?'

'No. I do not anticipate any trouble. You and your husband may stay on hand outside the door.'

With obvious reluctance, the nurse did as she was bidden.

Madeleine shivered, lying back as if exhausted while thinking rapidly. She must pretend to be unaware of their ruse. She said, 'Cornelius, thank goodness you are here. They do not seem to understand. My mother is ill and I must go to her.'

Cornelius laughed. 'I have no knowledge of your mother's state and care less. She may be dead already this past year, for all I know. Without her, I would have had no problem. My life would have been satisfactorily ordered.'

'You mean — the message was not true?'

What was she to do now? Somehow

she must get away.

'Naturally, I did not believe that you would listen to my plan willingly. How unkind you have been, my dear. To employ strong-arm bully boys for the express purpose of keeping me away. And from the house that should now be mine — and that I have cared for. Oliver gave me full responsibility for its upkeep; he gave no thought to it and never went there.'

'Cared for? But it was uninhabitable. Your friends had wrecked it.'

'Nonsense. It was fit for me and my enjoyment. It was always intended as my country retreat while you stayed in London.'

'But . . . ' Madeleine protested.

'See, I am not here to argue. Your actions in the past weeks — going against everything we had agreed — has shown me that you can hardly be in your rightful mind. That is why placing you here, with Nurse Herries and her husband, was the ideal solution. They have experience in caring for unwanted invalids here.'

'Unwanted?' Madeleine repeated faintly.

'Those with relatives happy to see them safely bestowed and then to forget about them. Out of sight, out of mind. Nurse Herries is expert and very discreet. That is why I employed her to look after you in the first place.'

'You would keep me here permanently?' Her horror was unfeigned.

'Only if I have to. But if you agree to the only sensible course of action, there will be no need for any of this unpleasantness.'

She swallowed. 'What course of action?'

'Marrying me, of course. After all, that is what you always intended. No great hardship, surely? Our stolen kisses did not give me that impression.'

She tried not to shudder. 'If it is a matter of money, I am sure we can come to some arrangement. Without your having to tie yourself to me.'

'Money? How could you misunderstand me so?' His tone was chilling, his eyes glittering. 'I want you. I love you — and have from first meeting you. I am deeply hurt that you should think otherwise.'

'Surely you will not force me to marry you, Cornelius! If you truly love me, you will let me go.'

'I do not care for that word. Force, indeed. But I assure you there is no point in resistance. I always get my way. You should realise that by now.'

She must keep him talking. She must buy herself time to think. 'Why, whatever do you mean?'

He laughed. 'You never suspected, did you? I am a ruthless opponent when crossed, my dear. You have more than once expressed surprise at your husband's change of character. Why he became so cruelly suspicious and unkind, with his strange allegations. His suspicions did not come from thin air. They came from me.'

She stared at him, stunned. 'But why?'

'Because Oliver's child was an

unwelcome complication. I want my sons to inherit the Corning properties and estates. *Our* sons. Not that interloper.'

Madeleine said sharply, 'It was you. You sent my baby away. You put him in that horrible place.'

'Ah, yes. But only on Oliver's instruction. My plan exceeded all my expectations. I merely planted the suggestions in his mind that the child was not his. I mentioned quietly in his ear that younger men had sought you out and were not rebuffed.'

'That was all wicked lies.'

'Of course. But he believed me.'

'How could you do that to Oliver? When he gave you employment and treated you so well? I thought you were close to him.'

He gave a harsh laugh. 'Treated me well? No doubt — as a dog is treated well. You thought him kind, but he always had a streak of cruelty. Stealing you and giving me employment so that I must witness his happiness. And yours. That hurt me, as he knew it would. He humiliated me purposely.'

'I do not understand. Why, then, did you stay?'

'Why indeed? For the inheritance, of course. At first, anyway. There were other cousins, you know, equally placed by blood. But Oliver always seemed to like me and promised that I would be his heir — but if I should wish to marry, I must seek his approval. As I duly did — and was told that he wished to meet you.'

'I knew nothing of that.'

'No. I did not tell you. I did not want you to be nervous on meeting him and maybe irritate him. He could be erratic in his likes and dislikes. But I was well rewarded for my consideration, was I not? He liked you all too well and decided to have you for himself.'

'That sounds so cold-hearted.' Had Oliver been capable of such conduct? Considering his later behaviour, maybe he had.

'And your mother,' Cornelius said

bitterly, 'had accepted me as a possible suitor when I told her of my expectations. But why take mere expectations when the original source of the wealth expresses an interest?'

Madeleine shook her head. 'That was dreadful, Cornelius. No wonder you were so angry.'

'Angry? That does not begin to describe my feelings. I was overwhelmed with an intense fury. I loved you. Was I to allow him to take everything that mattered to me, without protest? Oh, no. Lesser men might have taken themselves off to lick their wounds, but not I. Oliver had betrayed me and I planned my revenge. However long it took. Now you see how I will use any means to achieve my ends.'

He sat on the arm of a small chair, swinging one leg, smiling in arrogance. 'A great nuisance that you went against me and found the child again. But I am willing to be magnanimous. The child may be left where he is, where I suppose he will be happy enough — if you make a legal declaration that he is not Oliver's child and so cannot inherit.'

'No,' Madeleine answered, horrified.

He shrugged. 'Well — in that case . . .'

10

Madeleine did not want to hear his alternative. There could be no doubt. If he would only leave George in safety, she would sign anything. How could she put her child at risk? She said, more quietly, 'Very well, I will agree to that if I must. As long as you give me your solemn promise that he will never be harmed.'

He answered easily, 'Of course.'

She did not know whether to believe him. He had already demonstrated that his word was worth nothing. But what mattered, for now, was that he thought she believed him. It was the only way that she might gain any chance of escape.

She put her hands to her face. 'I am so confused. About everything.'

'That is why you need a strong man to look after you. And the estates you have gained: And according to our original plans. I am hurt and shocked that you sought to supplant me with that mealy-mouthed Franklyn fellow.'

'But who can I trust?' She managed a muffled sob. 'I am no longer certain of him.'

'You need not worry about trust. That is not a woman's function. I shall manage everything for you.' He paused. 'So now you are less than happy with your new love? Alas, how fickle we men can be. Well, I am not a vindictive man. I can make allowance for a woman's mistakes. Once the marriage is safely accomplished, I will forget all this ever happened.'

Hardly trusting herself to speak, she said, 'Thank you. I am very grateful.'

Obviously she must not marry him. Once that happened she would have no rights in law, except as Cornelius' wife. But she would have the three weeks of the banns — and there must be an opportunity to escape on the way to the church.

'Are you grateful?' He laughed. 'You will be eventually, I assure you. And do not worry, it will take place as soon as possible. I have procured a licence. And impoverished clergymen, who will act as instructed, are not hard to find.'

She said, beginning to despair, 'It must take place in a church. The vicar must not come to the house. It would not seem right, otherwise.'

He frowned and then nodded as if, having gained her agreement on the larger issue, he would indulge her on something that hardly mattered. 'I am sure that may be arranged.'

'Is there a church near here?' If she could only discover where they were.

'I expect so. There usually is.'

'Which parish is this?'

He smiled. 'We will find out when we sign the register, will we not?'

'Yes.' Did he believe her? Was she giving in too easily?

He said smoothly, 'Do not think that you will escape me this time. You betrayed me, cast me aside after all your promises. It will not happen again.'

'I never wished to betray you. I had no choice.'

He laughed. 'And we have made a full circle, as once again, you have no choice.' He leaned over her, his lips brushing her cheek. 'You see, although I welcome your abrupt change of heart, in my favour, I am afraid I have little faith in it. You will not be left alone for a single moment until my ring is legally upon your finger.'

* * *

She had hoped for three weeks, but she had only one night. She thought about refusing food and drink but without any nourishment, she would lack strength to escape. Nurse Herries laughed, seeing her reluctance. 'There is nothing in this. Not even to help you sleep — which I would have advised, myself. Mr Corning has great confidence in our abilities. As he should. We are very experienced in our care of invalids, as I told you. See, I will drink some myself.'

Madeleine took some, realising how hungry and thirsty she was. Nurse Herries unlocked the door and passed the tray outside. Then she settled down in a straight-backed chair, facing her patient. 'I should sleep if I were you, my dear. You will want to be fresh for tomorrow.'

'Tomorrow? What do you mean?'

Nurse pursed her lips. 'I am here to watch over you, not to talk.'

But surely, she must sleep sometime? Madeleine stared straight ahead, determined to stay wakeful.

Perhaps, she thought after a while, Nurse would be less alert if she thought Madeleine was asleep? Madeleine closed her eyes.

She opened them to see daylight around the curtains. Oh, no! How long had she slept? That wasn't what she had intended. But the hard chair was empty. She had succeeded after all. This was her chance. Heart beating, she slid out of bed and went quickly to the window.

Throwing back the curtains, she could have screamed in frustration. She was faced with stout metal bars. Beyond, there were the endless trees.

It would have to be the door. If only it might be unlocked . . . She was reaching out a hand to try it when the door opened and there was Nurse Herries, smiling. She held a cream-coloured dress over one arm.

'Ah, you are awake already. Good. We must be ready to leave soon. There is not much time.'

Madeleine drooped in disappointment. But she must not give up.

'Time? For what?' Although she already knew.

'For your wedding day, of course. Come, now. Is this gown not pretty?'

* * *

William took the familiar track at a canter, his heart singing. At last — he had accomplished his task. There would be no more secrets; he had won the right to tell Madeleine everything. She would be so happy — and well rewarded for her patience.

As he strode into the hall at Eastfield House, every sense alert for her presence, he realised that the usual atmosphere of peace and calm was lacking. Somewhere a child was crying fretfully. No one came out to greet him. He took the stairs two at a time, filled with a dread he could not name. As he reached the top, Ellen appeared, closely followed by Sarah.

He said, 'What has happened? Is George ill?'

'William! I thought — Yes — but we are almost certain it is nothing but a teething fever. George was a little fretful this morning so Madeleine did not take him with her to Brierley. But she did not intend to be long. I cannot understand her delay.'

'We thought you must be her,' Ellen said quietly. 'The fever is a little worse. She would wish to be here.'

'Have you sent for her?' A cold fear

was gripping his heart.

'I was about to. But . . . '

'She has not been herself lately,' Ellen said bluntly. 'Worrying herself sick over whatever has been withheld from her, in my opinion.'

'There will be an end to that now,' William said, cursing his father for being so stubborn and autocratic. He would never allow himself to be placed in such an impossible situation again. 'Even so, whatever her concerns, surely she would not have kept away from little George for more than an hour or so, in these circumstances? I will go and find her myself.'

At Brierley, the gig was still in the yard. He thought, *She is still here!*

But he knew with a lover's instinct that something was very wrong.

He threw himself from his horse and strode into the hall. He was met by Madeleine's housekeeper, frowning her concern.

'Oh, Mr Franklyn. Is there bad news? Of Mrs Corning's mother?'

His mind leapt to the only conclusion.

'There is nothing amiss with Mrs Corning's mother. I have just left her. What has happened here? And where is Mrs Corning?'

Fortunately the woman's explanation was clear and concise. 'But the groom who drove over with her took the horse from the gig, to accompany them. And they were to call at Eastfield House on the way.'

'They did not,' he said grimly. 'Which road did they take?'

'They set off in the direction of Eastgate village.'

'They would, of course. But they must have turned off.' And how much start did they have? If any harm had come to her, and after all she had suffered, he would never forgive himself.

Now he wanted only to gallop after that dark carriage at full speed but knew that would be futile. He must begin slowly, asking along the roadways, wherever they might have been seen. Swiftly he summoned all the grooms and workmen he had engaged to assist Madeleine, wishing there were more. They, too, must make enquiries in all the directions, as instructed — and return to meet him at Eastfield House within the hour.

The process seemed painfully slow, but villagers and cottagers could not be hurried as they scratched their heads, more than eager to help at the prospect of a few coins. At first, one or two thought they had seen the carriage but in the village itself, no one could tell him what he wished to hear. As he was coming away from the last cottage, he was met by one of his men on horseback. 'Come back to Eastfield, sir. We have news.'

'Tell me as we ride.'

'We found Robert, sir. Had been knocked from his horse and cracked on the head. But he's coming round now.'

'Is he badly injured?'

'We think not. And he's making sense.'

'Did he see which way they went?'

'To the east. The Falsborough road.'

The turn lay ahead. He thought quickly. Should he go that way immediately — or take time to question the man himself? This might turn out to be one of the most important decisions of his life. His success and Madeleine's safety could depend on whether he went swiftly, with what he had — or tried to gain more information first.

He thought, *They have a start — but a rider is faster than a coach. And so far I have nothing but a direction. There is a chance that Robert, the groom, might be able to tell me more. He might have overheard something of use.*

So acting against every instinct, he passed the turn and took the extra half mile — only to discover that his hope lay not with the dazed and regretful Robert, sitting in the kitchen while Sarah bandaged his head.

However Ellen ran out to meet him, flourishing a newspaper, her usual calm absent. 'Thank goodness they found you. I was so afraid they would miss you. I may know where she's been taken.'

'What? How?' He longed to believe her.

'Look at this. I found it when we were clearing Mr Cornelius' room, in London. It had fallen behind the chest of drawers and he must have overlooked it. See, this advertisement has been marked — and the name to contact: it is Nurse Herries.'

William skimmed over the small print: *a respectable couple will undertake to care for an elderly or infirm invalid* . . . His hope diminished. 'But this will be when Cornelius first employed Nurse Herries, surely?'

'No, see this bit — *in their own secure and secluded home, situated in pleasant surroundings*. And the date! Less than a month ago. Nurse Herries was working in London after George was born, in March.'

William read the advertisement again, a chill seeping through him. He knew of this practice, of course — who did not? Unwanted and inconvenient invalids, often with some disabling or embarrassing condition, could be disposed of and forgotten. Some of the people providing such a service might be caring and conscientious — but how many heartless relatives would trouble to check, beyond sending a regular payment?

Ellen was gabbling, 'I thought that too at first, when I found it. I didn't notice the date and I tried to tell Miss Madeleine about it as a matter of passing interest — and just a feeling I had that it could be useful. But we were interrupted and I pushed it into one of the boxes and had forgotten about it. If only I had realised sooner.'

'If only I had realised that Cornelius still posed a threat. I was too absorbed in what I had to do.' The man must have been planning this even then! An alternative, maybe, should Madeleine prove less than compliant.

'I'm right, aren't I? Mr Cornelius has taken her?'

William recalled how Cornelius had attempted to dispose of little George — and in a very similar fashion. 'I am afraid so. But he will not keep her. Thank you, Ellen. You have my undying gratitude.'

He thought, as he organised fresh horses for himself and three of the others, *I only pray we may not be too late*.

11

Madeleine glanced at the dress. 'I am a widow. Surely a more sober colour would be more fitting?' Anything to cause a delay.

'Mr Cornelius wishes this to be a new beginning — as if the old, false marriage had never been.'

Numbly, she allowed Nurse Herries to help her dress. She must be calm, alert for any opportunity. Perhaps she could refuse to take the vows. She could claim that there was an impediment. She would appeal to the vicar. Surely a man of the cloth would not make her go through with this against her will? All too soon her desperate thoughts would be put to the test.

Herries was outside the room, grinning, ready to grasp her arm once more. 'You had a quiet night, I see. I was at the door, on hand if needed.'

So even if she had not slept, there would have been little chance of escape. The net was closing around her. The dark, closed carriage in which she had arrived was waiting at the gate. As was Cornelius.

She said shakily, 'Surely we are not to travel together?'

'Indeed we are. I do not hold with idle superstition. I prefer to control this situation myself. Do not worry, Madeleine. Your happiness from now on is assured. I will make sure of that.'

It seemed that her guardians were to accompany them, Nurse Herries in the carriage also, and for once she was relieved. She did not wish to be alone with Cornelius. Mr Herries got up on the box with the driver. Now she was inside.

The journey was short and soon she was ushered out. Still the dark shadows of the woodland, and no sign of where the track ahead might lead.

They were at an overgrown churchyard. The rotten gate jammed and creaked as Herries struggled to push it open.

She said, 'This church is a ruin. Is it even used?'

'They still have burials, I believe. That need not concern us.'

'So how can we be married here?'

'It will be perfectly legal, I assure you — I would not take that risk. The place is still consecrated. It has suffered a lightning strike and a fire, but no one has troubled to repair it. The congregation simply go elsewhere.'

She stumbled on the step and his grip tightened. The church smelled of damp and burned timbers. She gasped at the dirt and dust of the interior.

'Come, my sweet. Soon the ceremony will be performed and we may go openly to somewhere you will find more to your taste.'

Madeleine did not reply. She was looking around her. Had the lightning struck the tower? She could see a narrow stairway leading upwards. If there was a tower, would there be bells?

If only she could attract the attention of good decent people who would help her . . .

The vicar was waiting at the altar steps. He was tall and unkempt and uneasy in his robes, as if he had not worn them for some time. She thought, *I have one chance. Show my intent too soon and I could spoil everything.*

She contented herself with a look of appeal. The vicar turned his head away, staring down at the prayer book in hands that trembled.

She said, 'Please, I would welcome a moment of quiet prayer, with the clergyman, alone. Before I take this momentous step.'

A mutter of growling dissent from Nurse Herries and her husband. She thought, *It is of no use*. But then to her surprise, Cornelius laughed. 'Most fitting, my love. Certainly you may have your quiet moment. We shall retire to the pews near the door.'

So there was hope. As they retreated, she murmured urgently, 'I beg your help. I am being made to go through this ceremony against my will. Please do not perform it.'

The vicar's face paled. 'You did not seem unwilling as you came in.' He spoke quickly, still without looking at her. 'Young women often do not know their own minds or understand what is best for them. Mr Corning seems an honourable man. Any woman of sense would be pleased to have such a husband to protect her and care for her.'

'You do not understand. He took my child from me; the child of my first husband. He has shown himself to be self-seeking and treacherous. You must help me.'

'I know you to be deluded, my dear. That is why you have a nurse in attendance. Accept this marriage as a blessing.'

Cornelius said, 'Enough of praying now.' He walked forward briskly. 'Let us press on.' There was a note of amusement in his voice. He had known, she thought, when he allowed it, what the outcome would be and that her appeal would fail. 'And do not, Reverend, be gazing around and awaiting a reply when we come to speak of impediments for I can assure you that there are none. We are both free to marry.'

'It is not what I want,' Madeleine cried, forgetting caution. 'Please, you cannot perform this.'

'Oh, but he can. He has been very well paid, you see.'

Madeleine put a hand to her face, feigning tears. She was filled with a cold fury. This must not happen! She must return to her baby — and William. Whatever had happened and whatever he was embroiled in, she would always love William. She knew that now, when it was almost too late.

Almost — but not quite.

Already, the vicar was gabbling through the service. 'Do you, Cornelius Maurice Corning, take this woman . . .'

'I do,' Cornelius replied abruptly.

'And do you, Madeleine Corning, take this man Cornelius Maurice . . . '

Madeleine threw back her head, collapsing onto the rubble-strewn floor.

'She is shamming,' Cornelius said angrily. Nurse Herries was slapping her face and wafting a small silver box under her nose. Madeleine smelled something pungent and coughed. Cornelius said, 'Just say the words over her. That will suffice.'

'I need to hear her speak.' So the vicar had come to her aid, after all.

Madeleine continued to gasp and choke.

'I'm sorry. Need air. The smell in here.'

The vicar said, apologetically, 'Quite understandable in a young woman of delicate sensibilities.'

Cornelius said sharply, 'Delay will do you no good, I promise you that. Pick her up. We will have the rest of the ceremony in the porch. Oh, leave her, man. I will do it myself.'

She made herself as heavy as possible

in his arms as he half-dragged and half-carried her. The tower was her only hope now. She pretended to regain her strength a little as they neared the door. Not difficult, as the stench was indeed overpowering and the fresh air most welcome.

Cornelius was obviously expecting her to try and run outside. He motioned to Nurse Herries to guard the outer door. As she stood up and they moved back a little, away from the porch, he relaxed. 'You see, there is no way out of this. You had best succumb to my will.'

Madeleine nodded, gasping, her lace handkerchief to her nose. Concealed in the glove and the handkerchief, she held a piece of rubble she had grasped when she fell. The vicar was standing before them, Cornelius standing beside her. The stairs were but a foot away. She did not look at them. The vicar said, 'Shall I start again?'

'No. Begin from where you left off. There will be no further swooning.'

'Do you, Cornelius Corning, take this woman . . . '

'I do. I have already said so.' His voice was sharp with annoyance.

'And do you, Madeleine . . . '

Swiftly, she swung the glove with the stone as hard as she could, striking Cornelius on the side of the head. His grasp loosened as he swayed back with an oath. It had to be now.

She darted away, through the tower doorway, banging the small door shut behind her. Weak and rotten as it was, it obeyed her — and there was a wooden bar to bolt it, which slid to. At last, she had a chance. Although she did not know how long the frail door would hold.

She fled up the uneven steps. She must reach the bells before the door gave way. Round and round. The stairs seemed never-ending. Her breath was coming in great panting gasps.

At last, here was an arch leading off the stairway. And a bell, one only, hung above her with a rope that disappeared through an open trap in the floor. It was not difficult to grasp it and pull. Nothing happened. She was not making the right movement to engage the clapper. How did a bell work? She tried again, pulling in a swaying motion, hoping to gain a momentum, until she thought her arms would give way. And at last the bell obeyed her. The noise seemed deafening. Surely someone must hear and come to see what was amiss? This was the age-old signal for alarm. But would they come here, or merely bolt their doors and hide to escape the danger? Or grab up their children and run? The noise of the bell was resounding in her head. Even so, she was aware of a dull thud below her as the door gave.

She dropped the rope. If there was anyone to hear her signal, it must have done its work. No purpose would be served by becoming trapped in the bell chamber. She must go onwards; if she could reach the top, she would be visible to anyone coming in answer to her summons. That way, she might have a chance. The steps were uneven; she almost tripped more than once: Her cream lace garment was smeared with dust.

There was a shout of anger and triumph behind her. She recognised Cornelius' voice. So she had not injured him badly. At least she had not killed him — but that meant her danger was acute.

Oh, no. The door at the top was shut. There was no handle visible. With as much strength as she could muster in her desperation, she threw herself at it and the timbers splintered and gave way. Thank goodness. She had done it. But there was no hope of bolting it behind her.

She looked round wildly. Now she was outside, up on the roof of the tower. But it would be of no use to stand here; the walls were too high; she could hardly see over them. Over there, at the far corner where the stones had crumbled away — she would be more visible there. And yes — surely there was movement on the roadway below. People on horseback.

The footsteps on the stairs were ever nearer. Almost upon her. She ventured along the uneven stones, disregarding her safety. They must see her now! She was right on the edge. She waved her arms. *Look up, please look up*. Swaying, she almost fell to the sickening drop below — but lurched sideways to where the parapet was in place. The stones wobbled beneath her grasp but held.

Someone looked up. She recognised the horse — and his dear face. 'William!' she cried in relief.

But already Cornelius was behind her.

'He shall not have you.' His face was contorted and ugly.

He followed the route she had taken but with even less care, arms outstretched to grasp her. He swayed as she had done and reached for the refuge of the same parapet, where the stones wobbled more ominously. He swayed again, losing his balance and the stones, thrust outwards by his greater weight, rocked and fell. And Cornelius fell with them.

* * *

Madeleine was shaking as she threw herself into William's arms. She was hardly aware of running headlong down the stairs, as if still trying to escape. She said, her voice fearful, 'Cornelius?' There was no sign of him here. He must have fallen on the other side.

'My men are attending to him. He will never trouble you again.'

She could hardly believe it. She was safe, in William's arms. Forever . . . But no. She gasped, remembering, and drew back.

'What is it, Madeleine?'

'You are not free. And I would never do anything to hurt Sarah. She has become my very dear friend.'

'Oh, my love. You will not believe

how much I wanted to tell you. But I had given my word. Believe me, it is the last secret I will ever hold from you.'

'Did you marry secretly? If so, you must honour your vows. I could not have it any other way.'

'No, I did not. Sarah was secretly married, yes — but to my brother. When he died and my father met Sarah and her sons for the first time, my father rejected them. He sent me to London, hoping I would find no evidence of the marriage. But I returned with the proof. My father was angry and still would not release me from my promise not to speak of it to anyone — but at last I have succeeded in persuading him. Sarah is a good woman and her elder son will become a fine heir to the estate.'

She felt like weeping with relief. 'I am so glad. How foolish I have been. I should have trusted you. Please forgive me.'

He said gently, 'You were under unbearable strain. But that is not all.

Once again, I must ask you to forgive me. There was one further promise I made that I could not reveal to you. My journey this week was in order to be released also from that promise. A journey that almost led to my losing you! If anything had happened to you, my life would have been worthless.'

'Why? Where did you go?'

'I have been to see your mother and sisters.'

'My mother! Is she well?'

'She is.' He smiled.

'Oh, thank God. But what do you mean? What promise?'

'I have at last convinced your mother of your innocence and reputation. She is now happy to be reconciled with you and your child. I was also able to address her major concern.'

'My mother will see me again?' Madeleine stared at him, still unable to believe that she was here with William and alive — still less able to adjust to this new information.

'I'm sorry. It is too much to tell you,

all at once. And yet, as I rode back, I vowed that from now on there will be no secrets between us.'

'Oh, William. As long as we can be together — I do not care. I love you. That is all that matters.'

He led her gently to a heap of broken stones. 'Sit down. You are shaking. But I must tell you. Some time ago, I came with my father to Falsborough. He wished to take the waters for his ill-health; he has suffered greatly since my brother's death, but will not own it. While we were there, he met the wife of an old friend. I was pleased, for he seemed to enjoy the lady's company while they shared memories of the gentleman in question and it improved his mood a little.' He paused, stroking Madeleine's hand. 'And then one day with my father out and I sorting some papers we had brought with us, I was surprised to receive a visit from the widow. Yes, you have guessed,' as Madeleine gave an exclamation. 'It was your mother.'

He continued, 'She had heard my father speak well, if grudgingly, of my abilities after my brother's death and that I would be visiting London to solve what he thought of as an attempted fraud. She begged my help and told me about you and how she had felt bound to sever all contact with you, lest she damage your sisters' marriage prospects.' He sighed. 'Even when I had never met you, that decision seemed harsh. And yet she was distressed about you, and I felt that I could not turn her away, although I had little hope of achieving anything useful.'

He paused, allowing Madeleine to absorb what he had said.

She smiled. 'So it was no coincidence, then, when I first saw you there on the street?'

'It was not. Please forgive me.'

'There is nothing to forgive.'

'I had to find some way of approaching you. I saw Mr Langholm turned away from your house, more than once, and despaired. But then, suddenly, there you were, leaving the house with your maid. I could waste no more time. I was by then exceedingly worried about you.'

'I could not have had a better guardian.'

'Your mother swore me to complete secrecy. So even when I had seen you moved from London — safely, as I thought — I could say nothing. But now she has released me from my promise. That was why I was away so long.

'Having seen my own father, I had to ride over to Rushwood.' He shook his head. 'If I had known the danger you were in, I would never have gone. Not at that time. I almost lost you.'

'But I am still here. It is all right. You came and saved me.'

'You saved yourself by your own courage and determination. Qualities that first led me to love you.'

'I cannot say what it was about you. I knew we had a connection, as soon as we exchanged looks.'

He smiled. 'And that is not all. I have returned with another promise; this time made by your mother and sisters.'

She smiled into his eyes. 'I think I may guess it.'

'Once you are out of mourning, my love, they will be most happy to attend our wedding.'

Tears of joy came to her eyes. 'Oh, William — it is everything I dreamed of and hoped for and thought I would never have.' She threw her arms around his neck, trying to thank him, but her words were lost as they kissed.

THE END

We do hope that you have enjoyed reading this large print book.

Did you know that all of our titles are available for purchase?

We publish a wide range of high quality large print books including:
Romances, Mysteries, Classics
General Fiction
Non Fiction and Westerns

Special interest titles available in large print are:
The Little Oxford Dictionary
Music Book, Song Book
Hymn Book, Service Book

Also available from us courtesy of Oxford University Press:
Young Readers' Dictionary
(large print edition)
Young Readers' Thesaurus
(large print edition)

For further information or a free brochure, please contact us at:

Ulverscroft Large Print Books Ltd.,
The Green, Bradgate Road, Anstey,
Leicester, LE7 7FU, England.
Tel: (00 44) **0116 236 4325**
Fax: (00 44) **0116 234 0205**